C000128984

MY DRAGON BODYGUARD

Broken Souls 4

ALISA WOODS

Text copyright © March 2020 Alisa Woods

All rights reserved.

No part of this publication may be reproduced, stored in a retrieval system, or transmitted in any form or by any means, electronic or mechanical, including photocopying, recording, or otherwise, without written permission from the publisher.

Cover by BZN Studio

ISBN: 9798624502758

My Dragon Bodyguard (Broken Souls 4)

She was abducted in the middle of the night...

Don't scream. Don't scream. Don't scream.

Jayda doesn't need to hear that.

And it makes Daisy cry.

But a scream is burning in my chest as they haul me to "the chair."

My tears mean nothing.

My soft begging is pointless.

They grab my arms and legs and strap me down and put that damn wand to my head... the one that reaches inside my mind and starts tearing it apart...

We escaped that nightmare—Jayda, Daisy and me—and now I just want my life back to normal. Forget those crazy aliens with their pointed ears. Forget all the screams. But as soon as I step on the set—my big chance as a Guest Star in a new medical drama —all of it comes rushing back. If it weren't for that hot new Production Assistant, I'd probably be in a psych ward by now.

The Universe is finally giving me a break.

Grace is desperate to put her life back together. Theo will do anything to keep her safe and help her heal… except tell her who he really is. And how he's the reason she was taken in the first place.

My Dragon Bodyguard is a steamy dragon shifter romance that'll heat up the sheets with love and warm your heart with dragonfire.

ONE

Grace

I HUDDLE IN THE CORNER, CURLED UP, TRYING TO stop the shaking.

"It's just the cold." My voice shakes, too. I can't even look at the freakish, padded operating-table-like thing in the middle of the room. It's warmer up in "the chair," off the glass-like floor, away from the smooth, glowing walls, but no way am I climbing into that thing voluntarily.

"Grace!" The voice comes through the grate in the wall—the vent connects to the next cell. "Girl, what did you say?" I can't see Jayda. I've never met her, face to face. I know her only from this place, this nightmare of a fucking place. The rich warmth of her voice is the only thing that keeps me sane.

"It's cold," I say, teeth chattering. But it's not

that cold. *I'm losing it.* "I can't… can't stop the… shaking." Jayda will know what to do.

"You are *strong*, girl," she insists. "We're going to make it through this, together. Just keep talking to me. I need to hear your voice, understand? I need to know you're okay. Talk to me, Grace."

"I'm—" A full-body shudder stops me, then I force out, *"I'm here."*

"You just keep holding tight."

"Hold tight, Grace!" The distant voice is Daisy. She's on the other side of Jayda's cell. Jayda helps Daisy, too, even though they come for her just like they come for us. Jayda's stronger than we are.

The shaking makes my foot tap, the one that's still wearing my sneaker. I lost the other one when they kidnapped me. I'd give anything for that shoe. Classic, red Converse sneaker. *Normal.* Not this insanity where aliens abduct me and… and… *Tap. Tappity. Tap-tap.* My foot's sending out some crazy Morse Code. H-E-L-P-M-E.

"Stop," I beg it, but it keeps on tapping.

"Stop what, honey?"

I can't answer. I'm focused on making my foot stop. It doesn't.

I hear Jayda sigh through the grate. "You need

some rest, that's all. Try to sleep. I know it's hard, but if you lean up just right against the corner—"

"Can't stop... the shaking..." I plant my bare foot on top of the shoe, pressing it into the floor. "Stop, God damn you!" I choke on the surge of scream climbing up my throat.

"Grace." Even Jayda's voice sounds shook now.

Suddenly, they're here. Two of them. They didn't use the door with no handle, but when they do... it just *disappears.* And reappears. Like them. Popping out of thin air with their gangly limbs and ugly faces and those awful, pointed ears.

"Noo!" I unfurl my crumpled body and bolt away from them. There's nowhere to go. My long hair flies all around me, blinding me in my desperate attempt to flee. One grabs me, his hands as rough as the scratchy alien words they use, telling me something I can't understand, but it's always the same. I thrash against his iron grip even though it's useless. *Don't scream. Don't scream. Don't scream.* Jayda doesn't need to hear that. And it makes Daisy cry. But a scream is burning in my chest as they haul me to the chair.

I can't help the little squeaks and sobs. I can't stop the muffled cry when the mechanical pinchers come out and *pin me.* They never pierce the skin, just hold you in a way you know you'll be cut to ribbons if you move. I freeze, whimpering. The aliens grab my arms and legs and strap me down. My tears mean nothing. My soft begging is pointless. But I can't help it. *Don't scream. Don't scream. Don't scream.*

Then the wand is at my head. Its cold crystal tip barely touches my skin, but somehow, someway, through the magic of whatever this fucking nightmare is, it reaches inside my mind and starts tearing it apart, piece by piece…

I scream like I'm turning inside out.

TWO WEEKS LATER

"You're wanted on the set," the 2nd Assistant Director says, but he's not talking to me.

There's a dozen of us in the waiting area, and we're all eager to get back on set, but the 2nd AD's just here for Ainsley. Everyone relaxes their Red Alerts as the two of them huddle and whisper. What does the AD want? She's a possible regular for the show, assuming the pilot doesn't get canned, so maybe they're adding lines for her? I hope my lines aren't already out of date. And Ainsley isn't taking my spot. I clutch my mini sides—the day's script on half sheets of paper—a little tighter in my hand.

Ainsley heads toward the set, and the 2nd AD shuffles over to me. My heart stutters. I'm out of the folding director's chair so fast it skids back behind me.

"You've been to hair and makeup, right?" he asks.

I nod quickly. "Wardrobe, too." I smile too much because, *Fuck, Grace,* it's obvious you've been to wardrobe. I don't walk around the streets of New York City in scrubs. I straighten my white doctor's coat.

The 2nd AD just checks his phone. "They're running through lighting again. Be ready."

I'm so ready, I'm starting to vibrate. I nod again, way too much, but he's already heading back to the set. I flash a bright smile at the other actors around the room—*be professional, be cool*—but most are already back on their phones, waiting.

Waiting is what actors do best! The pep talk in my head is in overdrive. I need to dial it back and save some energy for the scene. This is important. *Really* important. I need to bring everything I've got—

"You okay?"

I jolt inside my skin and turn—*who the fuck is*

sneaking up on me?—but it's just one of the Production Assistants.

I plaster a smile on my face. "I'm great! Doing good. Thanks." *Oh my God,* I'm going to blow this whole thing. I take the water bottle he's offering, to cover the awkward, then set my script pages on the table behind us because it's just too much to manage.

He smiles. "You were amazing yesterday."

"Are you serious?" I did mostly nothing yesterday. I laugh a little to burn off the nervous energy then cradle the water bottle with both hands. He must be new because I don't recognize him. And no matter how cranked up I've been these last three days on set, I wouldn't have missed a PA with those electric blue eyes. "That was like two seconds of long shot and a lounge bit. Today's my big scene. I mean, if you thought *that* was amazing…" I squeeze my eyes shut. *What the fuck, Grace? You're being rude.* I open my eyes, grimace, then make a desperate ploy for forgiveness. "I'm sorry, what's your name? I can remember my sixth-grade lines from Pirates of Penzance, but I can't remember names to save my soul."

He smirks. "We've just met."

"Oh, God." I press my fingertips to my forehead, wishing there was a reboot button for my brain. Or this conversation. Possibly my entire life. "Let's do another take, shall we?" I extend my hand. "Grace Tanaka. Otherwise known as *Dr. Lily Sato*, famed prodigy doctor from Johns Hopkins here to consult on a very special case. I should just stay in character. She's much cooler than I am."

"You seem to be doing all right." The sweet smile returns, and *whew*, he's hot. Young, probably twenty-five, so about my age, incredible bone structure, full lips, and a sexy scruff of beard even though it's 10 o'clock in the morning. His slightly swarthy look makes me think European Male Model, but I can't be sure what nationality. He's beautiful enough to be a lead, which makes me second-guess if he's really a PA.

I squint at him. "You're an actor."

He laughs. "I'm really not."

"But you want to be."

"No."

"In your deepest, darkest fantasies… totally on stage."

"Still no." He's smiling again.

I lift an eyebrow. "You're sure you're crew?"

"Positive." He leans in, conspiratorial. "I'm new here. Only been on set for three days."

I scrunch up my nose. "The set's only been up for three days."

He leans back and shrugs. Now I can't tell if he's joking or what. But this banter has drained some of the jittery energy from my body, for which I'm insanely grateful. So grateful, I feel like I should give Mr. Hotness a hug. Or possibly a *thank-you* handjob. After the shoot is done, of course. Except that would be highly unprofessional. And probably just my supremely-neglected libido talking. He *is* unnaturally gorgeous. I'm pretty sure any girl who can fog a mirror would have visions of getting on her knees in front of this guy.

I shut off the fantasies before they show up on my face. Then I make a show of unscrewing the cap of the water bottle he's brought me. "You're like a walking sedative." I take a sip.

"I'm sorry?" He gives me a look like I'm half-cracked.

Which, to be honest, is a fair assessment. "I mean, you're pretty to look at, and all, but not in a way that makes a person freak out. You're a calming influence. Just standing next to you, I feel more settled. At peace. Kind of like Prozac."

"Thanks?" But he's got a laugh around those pretty blue eyes, so I'm finally hitting my stride again. And it's true. I don't know why or how, but he's settling my nerves, despite the highly inappropriate sex fantasies he inspires. Maybe that's why—distraction in the form of hotness is keeping me from spooling up about the scene.

I recap the bottle. "Okay, now that we're best friends, you should really tell me your name."

He flashes that smile again, and mentally, I'm on my knees, unwrapping those tight-fitting jeans like what's inside is a present for my birthday. *Holy fuck, Grace, what is wrong with you? The man is just doing his job. Leave him alone.*

"Theo," he says with a sexy mouth that I'm starting to obsess about as well.

"Just Theo? Like Beyoncé? No last name necessary?"

"Theo Wyvern." His eyes light up. "It means dragon."

"Your name has a meaning? That's… *special.*"

He laughs, but in a cute kind of way. Cute. Hot. Calming. Exciting. This guy's a bundle of contradictions. Then he gets serious. "It's my family's name. Not like I got to choose it."

I lift both eyebrows. "Sounds like there's a story there." I take another sip of water and cap it again.

"Not really. Nothing you'd want to hear." He

drops his gaze like he doesn't want to talk about it. And it kind of stabs me because I get how family can *hurt*—even when they're amazing. Especially when they're amazing. Because there's nothing wrong with them—the thing that's wrong is *you.*

"Well, we *are* best friends." I hand the water bottle back to him.

"Are we?" He's smiling with his eyes again.

I shuffle dramatically over to his side, take hold of his arm, up by the bicep, and lay my head on his shoulder. I have to lift up on my toes because he's tall as well as gorgeous. "Have you forgotten already?"

"We literally just met." But I can hear the laugh he's holding back. And *damn* his biceps are like steel replicas of muscles under his Production Assistant black t-shirt. I resist the urge to feel him up inappropriately—is there a way I can *appropriately* feel him up? *No*—but the fantasy of peeling off his shirt just cannot be contained. He's incredibly ripped under there. I would spend a solid two minutes just running my tongue over the contours of his body. Because hotness.

"As I was saying… *best friends* understand there are some things that don't need to be discussed. Those deep, dark secrets of your past? Best friends help you bury that shit in the cemetery at midnight, am I right?" I peer up at him.

He's grinning down at me. "Are you always like this?"

I bat my eyelashes at him. "I have no idea what you mean." But then I release him because I really need my hands *off* the man or something inappropriate *will* happen. I smooth back Dr. Lily Sato's supremely-professional-yet-slightly-sexy hair, which is fashioned into a knot at the top back of my head, and I pray I haven't mussed it—Julie, the hairstylist, will murder me. "Okay, so I'm a little nervous. No chill at all. This is my first time as Guest Star."

"And this is a pilot, right?"

"Exactly." I pull in a breath and let it out slow, allowing the preternatural hotness of Mr. Theo Wyvern to wash over and calm me. "If the pilot is picked up, and if Lily Sato is a compelling and noteworthy character, *and* if they actually green-light a full season, I've got a shot at becoming a regular."

"Wouldn't that be a good thing?" His blue eyes are studying me, which gives me a flush of heat and naughty thoughts, but his words are ringing an alarm bell in my head.

"It would be *everything.*" I sweep a scouring gaze

over his headset and belt of assorted PA tools—extra battery clips, gaffer tape, and a flashlight. "Are you *sure* you're a Production Assistant?" Any PA would know that being a regular is huge—second only to being lead, and obviously that's already cast. At least for the first season. I narrow my eyes. "You're messing with me."

"Obviously." But his posture stiffens.

Weird. I *am* being kind of touchy, though. "Sorry, I'm just…" I squeeze my hands then shake them out, trying to stave off the return of the jitters. "I've done work before, a lot of it, you know, commercials and background and extras. A couple minor roles, just not at this level. This is my shot, and I thought I'd missed it—"

"Missed it how?" he asks, suddenly sharp-eyed.

"Oh. Um…" I glance away, to the door of the waiting room, willing the 2nd AD to come back and tell us it's time for the shoot. But he doesn't appear. I look back to Theo's too-intense scrutiny and feign nonchalance with a one-shoulder shrug. But my heart's pounding. "I just got sick is all. I landed the role before, um, I came down with the flu and was out a couple weeks. I thought maybe I'd missed the shooting window. But then the call came through, and I hadn't missed anything. I hurried in for the table read two days ago, and now we're shooting, and I'm just, you know, *excited!*" I grin, but I'm halfway to throwing up.

"Are you sure you're okay?" Even his eyebrows are pretty, especially all scrunched up with concern. And his voice has gone soft and sweet. "I mean, are you sure you're recovered enough from the, er, *flu,* for all this?" He gestures vaguely toward the set next door—the Art Department's created an entire fake hospital wing where the series will be shot if it gets picked up.

"Oh, *yeah!*" But it's too much, so I pull it back a little. "I'm fine. Just nerves. The camera rehearsal went great earlier. And it's not *that* tough a scene. It'll be good. Great, actually. Fantastic!"

Theo nods, but his scowl hasn't disappeared.

The 2nd AD appears at the door. *Thank God.* "All right, we're ready to roll. Everyone on set!"

I bounce on my toes and clap my hands with quiet, exaggerated enthusiasm. Then I reach out and squeeze his luscious bicep. *"Thank you.* I mean that. You're a fabulous distraction, which is just what a best friend should be."

That puts a smile back on his face, but then I'm rushing out to the set with everyone else, hustling to get to our marks. It's a crowded scene with a walk through the whole unit—nurse's station, patient rooms, lots of extras. It's a shuffle to get everyone in place. I nearly trip over the camera lines and dolly on my way to the room where Dr. Lily Sato is consulting on a case. She's young and female, so she's had to fight the Surgeon Boys' Club in pulmonary cardiology, which is her specialty. But she's also brilliant and has made a reputation for herself—and that reputation, plus a special presentation on a surgical technique she pioneered, has brought her to Chicago Hospital. She's nervous, just like me. She has to prove herself to this new set of doctors and staff. Again, *me*. All that is easy. It's keeping that tension under wraps, giving Lily that professional veneer, tightly controlled, but with a little touch of arrogance because my girl really is *all that*… that's the subtlety I've got to bring. The depth and emotional energy. I need to show Lily's got a whole lot under the hood—so much that the writers will be begging to give her more lines. Subtle. Powerful. A keen intellect but a wary understanding that so much is stacked against her. The entire profession is a minefield, but one she's skillfully navigated to this point because she's almost always the smartest one in the room. If she can just keep from stepping on a mine and blowing everything up...

Again... just like me. *We got this, Dr. Sato.*

I'm on my mark, waiting for lighting to finish their adjustments.

"Lock it up!" the 1st Assistant Director calls out. That's for everyone still off-set, warning them to keep quiet while we're rolling. I glance around—everyone's on their marks. The 2nd AD is fussing with the dolly for the camera. Theo, the sexy PA, is standing next to the director and the 1st AD, but he's hardly paying attention to them—instead, his pretty blue eyes are locked on me. He gives me a thumbs up. I flash him a look. *Of course, I've got this, don't be ridiculous.* Because I *am* Dr. Lily Sato now. We've got this all under control.

"Picture's up!" the 1st AD shouts. "Rolling, rolling, rolling."

The noise swells, the kind you'd expect in a hospital. No machines beeping—that'll be added in post—but bodies moving through their marks, muted conversations between nurses, doctors, patients being wheeled in, orderlies hustling through. The director's starting with a long shot then moving in to our part of the set. The two nurses in my room are checking the drip for the patient and adjusting the elderly man's oxygen mask. Dr. Sato is consulting, playing opposite Dr. Creskill, the resident in charge of the patient. We keep quiet until the camera dollies in. We'll have to shoot the reverse angles next, probably several runs through, but this first shot already has me on closeup, so I turn everything *on*.

"Admitted earlier today," Dr. Creskill says. "Swollen leg. High pain level. Deep Vein Thrombosis. Blood clot."

I'm scouring the patient's chart on a tablet like I'm fucking Sherlock Holmes, but I look up to glare at Creskill. I know what a DVT is. *Obviously.* But I keep it under control and turn to the patient, all empathy and concern. "What's your pain level now, Mr. Thompson?"

The patient removes the oxygen mask. "Hurts like hell," he wheezes.

The nurse urges him to put his mask back on.

My annoyance ramps up to serious concern. I shoot a murder look at the obviously highly incompetent Dr. Creskill. "DVT shouldn't be causing shortness of breath." I glance at the meds they have piping into the patient's arm. "Heparin drip?" I ask Creskill.

"Of course." He's getting huffy. Doesn't like me

questioning him. "We ran everything. CBC, BMP, Factor 5 Leiden."

I set down the tablet and lift the blanket covering the patient's leg—it's a fucking mess. Makeup did a hell of a job. I poke gently at the swollen calf. "CT scan?" I ask Creskill without looking at him, then snatch up the tablet again, looking for the results.

"Waiting on the scan."

"Well, it's here," I say, full of impatience because Dr. Sato knows this is very dire even if Creskill isn't quite on top of things. I briefly show him the scan then scour it myself, paging through a couple different views, all of the man's leg. I look up at Creskill. "Why haven't you done a chest scan?" I demand.

Creskill protests, "The shortness of breath is new—"

I pull up to my full height, my outrage pouring off me. "How long were you planning to wait? That clot could already have moved up to his lungs. He's a pulmonary embolism waiting to happen."

"Could you lower your voice?" Creskill hisses, red-face.

The patient is struggling with his mask, wheezing. "What's... what's happening?"

"We'll run another CT," Creskill snaps at me. "If it's moved, then we can send him to IR, get it treated endoscopically. No need to—"

"Doctor!" the nurse cries out. All the alarm bells of the medical equipment will be added in post, but we spring into action as if a five-alarm fire has just rung. The patient is slumped over, mask half off. The nurses are frantically scanning the equipment—the traces showing the patient's heart attack will also be added in post.

"No pulse!" the other nurse says, her fingers to the patient's throat.

"He's in V-Fib," Dr. Creskill says tightly, scanning the monitor. *"Bag him."*

I back off, letting them go to work on the patient, lowering the bed and the rails, removing his pillow, positioning him so they can try to resuscitate him. One nurse starts CPR, the other holds an oxygen mask bag over his face, pumping. My scowling for Creskill gives way to concern for the patient, my eyes wide and body rigid, staying out of the way so they can perform this life-saving dance.

"Paddles, charge to 200," Creskill calls out as he takes over CPR from the nurse.

The nurse grabs two shock paddles from the machine and rubs the faces of them together.

They're not hooked up to anything. There's no actual charge on those paddles. But something runs up the back of my spine—*a shiver.* A horrible dread crawls across my skin.

I almost say *Wait...* but the word stays frozen in my chest. My whole body is locked in place, suddenly clutching the tablet to my chest like it might protect me. *What the hell—*

"Charged," the nurse says, handing the paddles to Creskill. The other nurse has stripped the patient's robe, baring his chest.

"Clear!" Creskill shouts. The nurses jump back, hands in the air. He holds the paddles to the patient's chest and side.

The patient convulses. He arches up like he's being shocked with a million volts.

"No," I gasp. I have no air, so no one hears me. I'm not even on camera. I have no lines. Why am I talking? *I can't breathe...*

The patient slumps back to the bed.

Creskill shakes his head. "Epi, one milligram."

I don't realize I'm backing up until I'm against the wall. I can't make my lungs move. The nurse pushes fake medication into the fake patient's arm. *This isn't real. It's not real.* But I can't breathe. Can't move.

"Epi's in," the nurse says. They keep bagging him and performing CPR, but it's not working. He's dying. *I'm dying. Don't scream. Don't scream. Don't scream.*

"Charge again," Creskill says, his voice rising. The nurse charges the paddles, rubs them together, hands them to the doctor. "Clear!" They all jump back, hands up.

"No," I sob, but it's louder this time, air fighting its way in and then out.

The patient seizes, back arched, arms flopping like he's been electrocuted.

"No!" The scream is out of my mouth before I even know it's mine. Everyone turns. Something touches my arm. I jump so hard, I drop the tablet—my shield—and panic sends me flailing, scuttling, arms out, blindly groping my way out of the room because I can't see anything but a red haze of panic. *Get out!* is screaming through my head, but I barely make it out of the room before something trips me. I fall face-first on the floor, banging my forehead so hard that stars shoot across the red haze. I stay down, my body curled in a ball, everything shaking.

It's not real. Don't scream. I'm working full-time on getting air into my lungs. More stars swim in front of my eyes. I think I'm blacking out. *Breathe, Grace.*

Fuck! You have to breathe. One, long shuddering breath works its way into my lungs.

Hands touch me. I groan and flail against whatever's trying to grab me.

"It's okay. Grace! It's all right." The red mist thins enough that I can see brilliant blue eyes. *Theo.* His arm is like steel behind my back, lifting me up to sitting, but I'm still curled in a ball. He has something in his hand—a bandage—and he holds it to my head. "Can you hold this? Just hold it for a bit until the bleeding stops."

But I can't do anything. My hands are frozen, useless. All I can do is look at his beautiful eyes.

He grimaces. "Okay, you just hold tight."

"Hold… tight," I whisper. That's all the air I have.

"That's right." His eyes are so intense. *Focused.* "I'm getting you out of here." And then I'm up off the coldness of the floor and tucked against the warmth of Theo's chest. The rest of the hospital is a blur as he carries me away, somewhere, I don't know where. I don't care. All I know is that each jostle, each bump ekes a little more air into my lungs. Each breath relaxes my cramped muscles a tiny amount. I manage to open my hand, which is curled against his chest, just enough to grab hold of the fabric of his shirt.

I bury my face in it. "Hold tight," I whisper into him.

His arms squeeze me a little harder.

TWO

Theo

I really thought she'd be okay.

Grace is so strong—*so dragon spirited*—she seems like a goddess of fire that nothing can touch. Even unspeakable torture at the hands of dark elves who were literally determined to *destroy her soul* seemed to slide right off her.

But now she's huddled in my arms, covered in her own blood, and all I can think is, *Theo, you're a fucking idiot.* No one survives a trauma like that unscathed. They can hide it or ignore it or run away from it, but only for so long. I should have seen the crash coming. Was I just stupid, or did I *willfully* not see the signs? That would be so much worse—the only reason I'm here is to watch over her, and I'm fucking that up completely.

Grace drew the short straw in soul mates with me.

We're perched on the curb outside the set, the morning sun blazing down hot on us. I've settled Grace in my lap, and she still has a grip on my shirt, eyes squeezed shut. Camping on the sidewalk isn't ideal, but it's away from the set and easy for the paramedics to find us. Someone called it in. I waved off everyone else who was crowding us, worrying and wanting to help. We're just outside the studio now but still back from the street, at the edge of the minuscule parking lot. The traffic noise and sunlight seem to be settling her. But she's too damn quiet.

And her head is still bleeding.

I take the bandage someone scrounged from the set and hold it to the gash on her forehead. Her brown eyes open and lift until she's looking in mine. *Holy Magic, she's beautiful.* Even with the blood all over her face and chest, and the bun on top of her head let loose, long hair wild and tangled. She looks like a fierce warrior goddess who's just slain an entire legion of demons and lived to tell the tale. Only, in reality, *she's* hurt... and because I failed to see this coming.

I check her wound—it's starting to clot. "How are you feeling?" A siren wails in the distance.

She swallows, and her skin seems to gray before my eyes. "Dizzy." She squeezes her eyes shut again like it cost her something to talk.

My stomach's one hard knot. "You took a pretty hard blow. Might be a concussion. The paramedics will be here soon."

Her eyes pop open, filled with that same panic she had while tearing out of the patient's room on set. "No." She shakes her head, violently, then winces. A small whimper escapes her, and the sound stabs right through me. She grabs harder onto my shirt.

Every fiber of my being is screaming, *Fix this!* If only I knew how.

"Grace, it's okay." I cover her hand with mine, holding it to my chest, trying to tell her without words that I'm not going anywhere. I'm sticking with her through this, whatever *this* ends up being. That part is without question. It has something to do with the fact that we're two halves of the same soul. I wouldn't call it *love*—more like *instinct*. But the instant the witch, Alice, used her magic to pair me with Grace, revealing the connection we already had, being two parts of a whole, I knew I would do anything to keep Grace safe. The way you'd protect a baby you found crying in the forest. Except Grace isn't a child. More precisely, how I'd save my own hand from burning in a fire. Grace is *part of me,* and the need to make sure she's okay is as powerful as the survival instinct itself. Maybe more so because I'm sure I'd rush into a burning building to save her.

Which is such a strange thing to feel for someone you don't even know.

In theory, I'm supposed to fix that, too. Not that I'd mind getting to know her. She's an incredibly beautiful woman—almost painfully so. I feel a little weak every time I look at her like she belongs on some different level I'll never ascend to. But she's a complete stranger who knows nothing about any of this—or anything about me. Grace is a mysterious, beautiful, broken stranger I'm supposed to somehow care for, heal, then fall in love with. That's the fairy tale I've heard all my life.

Reality is so much more complicated.

The ambulance, F.D.N.Y. emblazoned on the side, rumbles into the far side of the parking lot, killing the siren, but not before it catches Grace's attention. She whips her head up, lips parted, chest suddenly heaving. There's blood all over her white doctor's coat. I try to gently pry her hand from my shirt, but she just grabs harder and shakes her head.

I don't know why she's panicking anew… then it clicks. And I want to smack myself. *Ambulance. Medical drama.* The elves fucking tortured her on a nightmare chair with metal appendages that came up from the bottom, like an overturned surgical beetle. I got a good look at it during the rescue, and the thing gives *me* nightmares. Apparently, anything medically-related is flashing her back. Which is bad news for an actor in a medical drama. But that's not important right now…

"They're just going to check you out," I try. "Make sure your head—"

"*No.*" She lets go of my shirt and scuttles away as the ambulance rolls up.

"Wait!" I go to her, trying to get her back in my arms or at least holding my hand, but she wants nothing to do with me. She's on all fours on the sidewalk, trying to both crawl away and work up to standing. She's in no shape for any of it. "Grace, you're just going to hurt yourself." I should simply pick her up, but it feels wrong. I decide I don't care. I'm not letting her take another header into the concrete.

I slip an arm around her waist and hoist her up from the ground. She's so light, it's ridiculous, but I can easily hold her up even though her legs are buckled. She squirms, not fighting me just twisting around so she can grab hold of my shirt again.

She pulls me to her until I'm nose-to-nose with her panic-filled face. "Theo, *please*. I can't. *Not this.*" Her words tumble out fast, her breathing erratic. "Call Jayda. She'll come for me. She'll take care of me."

"Jayda?" *Whoa.* Could they still be in touch after the—

"*Please,* Theo." The panic is making her shake.

Two paramedics hop out of the ambulance, one coming for us, the other going around back, probably for a stretcher.

I put up my hand, the one not wrapped around Grace's waist, to stop the paramedic. "Hold on."

She looks confused then glances at the studio door behind us. "We only got a call for one injury. Possible concussion. Are there more?"

Grace is so agitated, she's climbing my body, arms around my neck, leg hooked over my hip. Having her all over me like this would be hot as hell, except she's close to a full-blown panic attack. I've got a strong grip on her waist, so she can't slip out. I use my free hand to cradle the back of her head and tuck her face into my shoulder. She burrows in, shutting out the ambulance, the paramedic, everything.

"It's okay," I whisper to her. Then I look straight at the paramedic. "They're not going to take you anywhere."

Her eyebrows hike up, taking it all in, but then she signals to the other paramedic to stay back. He freezes with the stretcher halfway out of the ambulance.

Grace has a death grip on the back of my shirt. "My phone," she whispers into my neck, where her face is still buried. "Jayda's my emergency contact."

I know exactly where her phone is—it's my job to make sure everyone leaves them in the waiting area. The director's a tyrant about no phones on set. And unfortunately, I took off my headset before the take, so I can't call another PA to bring it. I briefly map out the studio in my head—I've been traipsing through every inch over the last three days, running errands for everyone—and I think I can get there without going past the fake hospital that is the set.

"All right, here's what we're going to do," I say to Grace and the two paramedics. I dip my head to speak softer to Grace. "We'll go get your phone from the waiting area. We'll call Jayda. And she'll come take you home. Okay?" She's still clinging to me. I can feel her shake. "You with me on this, Grace?"

She hesitates then nods into the crook of my neck.

"Here we go." I lift her up by her slim, little bottom and hook her legs behind me. She locks them, hard, keeping her head tucked. Being dragon means I've got more strength than your average guy, but Grace is all slim bones and lean everything—carrying her is not a challenge. I motion with my chin for the paramedics to follow, then I walk us back inside. The phone might be enough to calm her down for an exam. They *need* to check her out. I may not have a ton of experience outside the lair, and definitely not with injured humans, given dragons are pretty self-healing from even grievous injuries, but even I know Traumatic Brain Injury is a thing and head wounds are nothing to mess around with. We sneak around through the Art Department, me glaring at the few people who look like they might say something, and I see the red light is on down the hall, so they're rolling again. Which is good—that's fewer people in the waiting area. When we get there—me, Grace, and the two paramedics—the only person there is Billy, one of the PA's, cleaning up the craft service. I wave off his questioning looks and carry Grace straight over to the bin where we keep the phones. I snag the container then walk us to a table, where I set down the phones and carefully ease her onto the molded plastic surface. It's steady enough to hold her.

She's still clinging to me.

"I gotta set you down, Grace. My arms are getting tired." Complete lie, but it works. She releases her arm-lock around my neck and settles her butt back on the table, but she still has a hand flat on my chest. Right over my heart. Like she needs that connection to be okay.

Which is fine. I'm not going anywhere. I stay close, standing between her legs as I rummage through the bin and come up with her phone—the case is a picture of Shakespeare in pink shades with the words, *You are a saucy boy.* She snatches it from my hands, but hers are still shaking.

I wait until she gets it unlocked then lean in. "Want some help?" I ask softly.

The paramedics are standing by, having a silent conversation. But they're being cool, waiting for things to stabilize. I wish I knew how long we had— the director didn't have much more scene to get through. Soon, he'll want to call a break to set up another shot, and then everyone will be back here.

Grace is trying to bring up Jayda's number, but she keeps hitting the wrong buttons. She closes her eyes briefly, takes a deep breath, then opens them and hands the phone to me.

"I got you," I say, then rapidly search her contacts for Jayda and punch in a message. *This is Grace's friend. She's taken a fall on set and is pretty shook. She wanted me to text you. Can you come?* Then I add the address of the studio. I have no idea if Jayda will even see this, but just sending it has Grace's shoulders relaxing. I hand the phone back. She glances at the message then holds the phone to her chest, eyes closed. When she opens them, she looks deep in my eyes but doesn't speak.

I dip down and say, "You can thank me by letting the paramedics check you out."

Her right eyelid twitches, and her eyes glaze, staring straight into my chest but not like she sees me... then she nods. I put a hand on her knee just so there's still contact between us, then scoot to the side to make room for the paramedic. She doesn't have a nameplate or a badge, just patches that say PARAMEDIC and FDNY. She's short and compact, with warm brown skin and sharp brown eyes. Her hair is pinned up in a no-nonsense style, and she's all business with Grace. The male paramedic is her physical opposite—white skin, tall and lanky, his hair the kind that stands up even when you've combed it. He's holding back and clutching a bag of something, but the stretcher is thankfully still in the ambulance.

The female paramedic tips her head to catch Grace's attention. "Hey there. My name's Alicia, and I'm here to help you. What's your name?"

"Grace Tanaka." She has to swallow to get it out, but her voice is surprisingly steady, just soft.

Alicia frowns, glancing at Grace's doctor's coat. *Dr. Lily Sato* is half covered in blood but still visible.

"That's her character," I toss in. "Her name *is* Grace."

Alicia peers at her head wound but doesn't touch her. "How old are you, Grace?"

"Twenty-five."

She dips her head to catch Grace's gaze. "Do you know what town we're in?"

Grace squints like she's slightly annoyed. Or maybe confused. I can't tell. "Manhattan."

"Do you know what day it is?"

Grace's eyes widen, then she sneaks a look at her phone. "Friday," she says, voice stronger.

Alicia smirks. "I'd be screwed with that one, too."

The tension in Grace's shoulders seems to ease. "I'm fine. Just fell and cut my head." She dabs at the wound and seems to realize for the first time how much blood is everywhere. *"Fuck.* Wardrobe is going to kill me."

Alicia laughs a little. "I think you're going to be fine, but I'd like to check your pupils if that's okay?"

Grace nods her assent.

Tension gushes out of me like a waterfall. *She's going to be okay.* Not just because the paramedic says so, but because Grace is coming back to normal. Well, maybe still a little freaked. But normal enough to get medical care.

Alicia fishes out a penlight from her pocket then flicks the light at Grace's pupils. "Can you tell me what happened just before your injury?" she asks casually.

Everything in me stiffens.

Grace's lips press together, but she's letting the paramedic finish the pupil check.

"Your pupil response is good." The paramedic hesitates and glances at her partner, then asks, "Do you remember what happened before you fell?"

Grace nods, but her lips are still pressed tight.

"It's okay if you don't want to talk about it," the paramedic says with a glance at me. "I'm just trying to check your memory, all right? What's the last good thing you remember before you fell? Just so I know you're not experiencing some temporary amnesia."

Grace sits a little taller. "Theo was helping me. Calming my nerves before the shoot."

Alicia gives me an approving look. "Looks like you're in good hands, then. Are you experiencing any dizziness, ringing in your ears, or nausea?"

"No." She sounds stronger.

"Headache?"

Grace presses her fingers to her temple. "Yeah. A little. I mean, I did smack it on the floor." She frowns. "I think it was the floor."

"You hit the dolly on the way down," I throw in with a small smile.

"Oh, God." She rubs her temple then looks disgusted at all the blood on her hand. She gives her phone over to me then uses her doctor's coat to wipe it off.

Alicia beckons the other paramedic over. "Frank's going to get you cleaned up, okay?" Then she turns to me and lifts her chin like she wants to talk separately. I give Grace's knee a squeeze and wait—I'm not going anywhere if she still needs me —but she's ignoring me and looking with interest at the bag Frank has set on the table. As he gets busy unpacking, I shuffle over to where Alicia's moved a dozen feet away.

Far enough for her lowered voice not to travel. "Do you want me to bring her in? We can arrange a psych eval—"

"What? No. She's fine." I keep my voice down too.

Alicia's expression is vastly less impressed than a minute ago.

"Okay, maybe *fine* is a little strong. She's… going through some things. Right now, I'm mostly concerned about her having a concussion."

Alicia's disapproval lightens a little. "She's alert, responsive, and aware. Doesn't seem to have any memory loss. No major confusion or dizziness or nausea. I'm guessing she's fine, but that's just a guess. She needs someone to stay with her. If there's no worsening of symptoms, no headaches or extreme drowsiness, no memory problems, in the next twenty-four hours or so, she'll probably be fine. She should still follow up with her doctor, but if she has any strange symptoms, even things I haven't mentioned, you need to get her to the ER."

I pray it doesn't come to that. They'd have to sedate her or something. She already looks better, mostly because Frank has cleaned a lot of the blood off her face. A butterfly-shaped Wonder Woman bandaid is now holding the gash on her head closed.

Alicia digs a card out of her pocket and hands it to me. "In case you change your mind about that psych eval."

"Thanks." I pocket the card. Who am I to tell Grace she needs to see a shrink? My gaze is drawn back to her blood-spattered form on the table. I'm Grace's dragon soul mate, the one who's supposed to romance her into mating, fulfilling the hopes of my parents and my people. But I'm also the reason she was kidnapped and tortured. And somehow, I'm supposed to *also* be the guy who fixes everything and helps her move on when I barely know what I'm doing with my own life. It's completely fucked up.

Maybe *I'll* go see the shrink.

Suddenly, a tall black woman tears through the waiting area doorway. She's out of breath, frantically scanning the room, heels clutched in her hand, sneakers on her feet, in a dark-gray impeccably-tailored suit, but her black silk blouse is half untucked from her slacks. She sees Grace and gasps something like *Oh, my God* and sprints across the room.

"Grace, honey, oh *Jesus,* what happened to you?" It's all a gush, but Grace doesn't have time to answer because the woman—who can only be Jayda—has scooped her into a hug that lifts her halfway off the table. Then she quickly releases Grace and, still holding her heels in one hand, grabs her by the shoulders to give her a rapid-fire looking-over. Frank cleaned her up, but there's still blood all over her doctor's coat—and now probably some on Jayda's fancy business attire.

"Is she all right?" Jayda demands of Frank.

"She's going to be fine." His tone is gentle, probably meant to be soothing.

"She does not *look* fine." Jayda's wrath makes Frank lean back. "That's a *lot* of blood. What the fuck happened here?" She's ramping up like she thinks Grace is getting substandard care, and I'm afraid it will affect Grace. But then her voice softens. "Jesus *Lord,* Grace, honey, what happened to you?"

Grace puts her hand over Jayda's on her shoulder. "You came." She breathes it out like Jayda's touch alone is calming, no matter the panic on her face.

"Excuse me? *You texted me.* I am *here* for you." Jayda moves her hold on Grace to her hands. "Even if I had to sneak out of a meeting, sprint four blocks, and knock some lady's cappuccino mocha all over her blouse. Now tell me what happened."

But Alicia's moving in to manage the situation. "She fell and took a knock to the head, but there's no sign of concussion at this time."

I hover at the edge of the tight circle around Grace, ready to jump in to support Alicia if needed. Jayda's rapidly scanning her paramedic uniform, and I can see the fierce intelligence in her eyes— she's assessing, deciding if this person knows what she's talking about or if Jayda needs to take things into her own hands. And Jayda Williams is a woman who gets things done. I've seen her profile. She's older than Grace, thirty-two if I recall correctly, but that's not why. She's a Wall Street prodigy—mergers, acquisitions, and high-flying corporate business.

"No concussion," Jayda echoes back to the paramedic. "But a whole lot of blood."

"Head wounds bleed a lot," Alicia says, calmly. "Usually looks a lot worse than it is."

Grace tugs on Jayda's hands to bring her back. "I'm fine. I just… I needed you here. I thought I was…" She takes a deep breath. "The hospital scene was a lot." She's still shaking a little.

Jayda's lips press together, and she seems to struggle for words. Then she leans closer, squeezing Grace's hands. "You're going to be okay." It's so soft, I almost can't hear it.

Alicia glances at me, then lifts her chin to Frank. He's already put his clean-up supplies back in his bag. "Okay, we're rolling out," she announces. To me, she says, "Just keep an eye on her, like I said."

"Will do." I give her a tight smile. "Thanks."

Alicia and Frank head for the door.

Jayda releases Grace and parks her hands on her hips, giving me that same scouring look-over. "I'm sorry, who are you?"

"The one who texted you." That gives her pause, so I quickly explain. "They said Grace needs someone to watch over her for the next twenty-four hours. I can do that. But I think we should get her home."

Jayda's assessment drops into a scowl. *"We?"*

"Theo's a good guy." Grace has shucked off the blood-spattered doctor's coat, leaving just her scrubs, which is fine, but she's also trying to stand, which kicks up my heart rate a notch.

Jayda sees it too. "Where you going, girl?" Her hands are up like she might catch Grace if she fell. Which maybe she could—Jayda's tall, lean, and radiates the physical confidence that comes from someone who's strong and knows how to use her body—but I don't want to take the chance of Grace falling again.

I swoop in and slide my arm around Grace's waist.

"I'm fine!" she protests, but she's not—she sways, and her hand presses flat on my chest again.

"How far is your place?" I ask pointedly. I can't let on that I know where she lives, but it's a good mile away. And one thing is clear from just the two weeks I've been in New York City, looking out for her, is that everyone walks everywhere. Or takes public transportation. I look to Jayda. "Can you call us an Uber?"

She purses her lips, but her hand's already digging in her pants pocket for her phone. "We'll talk about this on the way."

But Grace is holding onto me, and I don't think she'll easily let go. I hate that she's hurt, but it opens up a possibility like a plot twist on her *Scrubs of*

Chicago show—I've got a way to get close to her now. I'm supposed to win her love to seal the mating. I should insist on watching her—*closely*—and then seduce her. It's how this story is *supposed* to go, regardless of what the main character—me—wants.

All I want is to make sure she's okay.

But I don't get to decide. I'm not the writer of my own story, not really. Not when I'm paired with a single soul mate in the entire world and the fate of my people rests on me doing my duty. I'd halfway hoped an escape would present itself. Some amazing *Deus ex machina* plot device that would solve my unsolvable problem in some wildly improbable way. I'd be free. Grace would be happy and whole. We'd each merrily go our separate ways.

Instead, a trap door just opened in front of me… and I have no choice but to walk straight in.

"Let's go." Jayda's in charge, phone in hand, leading the way back outside.

My arm's firm around Grace's waist as I shuffle us along behind.

THREE

Grace

I'M AN EMOTIONAL WRECK.

Just straight-up emotional carnage so bad, I'm not even sure what I'm processing right now. Relief that Jayda's sticking with me all the way home. Guilt that I had a freaking *panic attack* and both she and Theo had to leave work to take care of me. The shakes from that still haven't left my body— Theo practically carried me in and out of the Uber. I'm still leaning on him, his arm firm around my waist, as the three of us ride the elevator to my apartment. The heat of his body touching mine plus the hard steel of his muscles tosses *lust* into the pile of manic emotions wringing out my heart. But most of all, there's an abyss opening up at my feet.

I failed. I couldn't hold it together for even one

scene. I utterly, completely, totally, ambulance included, fucked up my one chance to make everything right.

That's the dizziness that keeps coming back in waves. It's not the knock to the head. It's that I'm once again *Grace the Epic Failure*, and it's almost too much. On top of... *everything else*... why can't I do this one thing right? As we reach my apartment door, the jittery feeling of being on the edge of the abyss makes me cling harder to Theo's shirt.

He frowns. "Do you have keys?"

I swallow down the feeling of an endless void reaching up to grab me. "Keyless entry. App on my phone."

"Really?" He pulls my phone from his pocket, but we're already close enough for it to auto-detect. The door clicks open.

Jayda raises her eyebrows and pushes open the door. She hasn't been to my apartment. It's in Chelsea, and my parents are, well... *rich* is probably the least offensive term. The apartment is over the top because Mom insisted. She's an artist, and she has a certain taste and... I didn't want to get into all that, so Jayda and I just met at her place in Midtown or out for coffee. We've only seen each other three times face-to-face in the city and never here at the apartment. Judging by Jayda's face now, that was the right call.

"Holy shit, Grace." She's stepped through the foyer and out to the great room. It's huge, as far as apartments in the city go. Columns hold up the ceiling for the wrap-around windows with a view of Manhattan. The décor was done by one of Mom's friends—someone famous in the interior design world—and has a spare feel like they were afraid to use too much furniture. The apartment building itself is one of Dad's award-winning designs. Mom's sculpture sits at the end of a room-spanning couch that could easily hold ten, but only ever has been occupied by me and Mari, my sister, while we binged on Netflix shows she liked. Dad installed a TV screen that rolls down from the ceiling—he loves that feature, but he and Mom never come around to hang out. Just Mari. She always picked out the shows, and I would critique all the acting, and she would punch me in the arm and say I was terrible and spoiled everything and I would do it more. We ate so much popcorn on that couch. Despite the housekeeper's best efforts, there were always kernels in the cushions.

Before Mari died, of course. Now the kernels are gone.

The abyss is Vanta-black, so deep and filled with emptiness, I'm surprised Theo and Jayda don't feel its vacuum sucking all the warmth from the room.

Jayda turns her amazement at the apartment back to me. "I thought you were an *actor.*"

"It's family money." My words are cotton in my mouth. *Family.* There's just three to that number now, not four. Jayda comes closest to being the kind of sister-friend I would bring here… and I still didn't. *Couldn't.* Not until now, when I have no choice because I'm having some kind of mental breakdown.

Theo, to his credit, barely gives the place a glance—his beautiful eyes are locked on me, his face all furrowed concern. "Do you want to sit over here?" He guides us toward the couch. I still haven't let go of him, not on the whole trip home.

"Okay." I curl up in the corner—the place where the two fifteen-foot halves of the taut sky-blue fabric meet. It's my spot. Mari would tease me about it, but it was my corner—my back to the city, the screen our whole world when it scrolled down. It was like being in my own, safe, cozy world of make-believe, just Mari and me. She would always sit to my left…

Which is exactly where Theo settles. I forgot to

let go, and now he's on the couch with me, arm resting behind me, his big hands—so big; like he's a puppy that hasn't quite grown into them— smoothing back the wildness of my hair, so it falls behind my shoulders.

I look at him with amazement. How is this beautiful man so sweet? And kind? I'm a stranger to him, and he's just taking this all in stride like he has women falling to pieces around him on the regular.

It intrigues me, even in the mire of my own misery, looming at the edge of the abyss.

Jayda's giving him the side-eye. I can't figure out why.

"Thank you... *Theo*... for helping get Grace home." She says it with a tone that's mostly *fuck you*. "But we're good now. You can go back to work."

Theo doesn't move a muscle. "You're the one who probably needs to go back to work. No one's going to miss me on set. And Grace needs someone to stay with her. Paramedics said twenty-four hours."

Jayda's not happy, but the thought of twenty-four hours of Theo on my couch is beating back some of the bleakness. Would he really do that? For someone he just met? Is this guy a saint? Or is it something else?

Jayda seems to suspect *something else.* "Look, no offense, but I don't know you—"

"It's okay, Jayda." I haven't spoken much during the ride, so it stops her. And I know about Jayda's past with men. We've talked—*a lot*—the way I've only ever talked with Mari. Jayda was burned in the worst way, and I don't blame her for being suspicious of anyone with a penis. There are monsters out there. I know that all too well, even though I've led a Lucky Charms life where the monsters never bothered me. At least, not the human kind. I don't know why. Maybe I'm just that prickly and weird, even the bad guys don't want a bite. But I've got a deep-down feeling—Mari called it my Gut-o-Meter—and it says Theo's not that way.

Jayda comes closer and kneels in front of my corner. "Grace, honey, I *do* have to get back. They're lighting up my phone, wondering when I'll return to that damn merger meeting. The report for the private equity guys is due tomorrow, and we're only halfway through the diligence review—" She cuts herself off, grimacing and grabbing hold of my hand. "I can be back here tonight. Can you hold tight until then? *Without* a babysitter?" She gives a cold look to Theo, who's stone-faced through all of this. "If not, I can find someone to watch over you."

I squeeze her hand. "I'll be okay. But I want Theo to stay. Just in case. I don't want to pull you out of an important meeting just because I have another drama-queen swoon." Jayda gives me a look like she's not buying my bullshit. And it's stupid to make light of it, but I'm jittery, too many emotions swirling around in me, and that's what comes out. *Wise cracks. Sarcasm.* I know what I do. I just can't help it right now. I take a breath and try to be real. "I need someone here. Just for a little while." It wouldn't have to be Theo, but I feel so unmoored, I really do feel unsafe being alone. And it can't be Jayda. She has a life—a real life and a real job and important things to do. Unlike me, who's basically flamed out on the only thing I've ever been good at. Theo can be my distraction... and maybe he'll keep me out of the abyss.

Jayda purses her lips, and uncertainty flickers in her eyes. She stands and peers down at Theo. "Seems like we should exchange phone numbers, Mr...?"

"Wyvern." Theo scoots forward, digs out his phone, and hands it to her.

While Jayda enters her contact info or maybe texts herself, she gives me a soft look. "You *use* that emergency call on your phone if you need it. You hear me?"

"Promise." I give her a smile that's not too weird. Maybe.

She hands Theo his phone, hugs me fast and hard, then heads out. I wait until I hear the door click, then turn to Theo, but he's smirking at his phone.

"What?" I peek at it, so he shows me. It's a text Jayda sent to herself. *I don't know who you are, Theo, or what your game is, but if you hurt Grace in any way, I will fucking murder you, and the body will never be found. I am not kidding. Do not underestimate me.*

I fight a hiccup of a laugh. "I wouldn't."

He stows his phone. "You wouldn't what?"

"Underestimate her." I'm totally serious now. "She's the strongest person I know."

"I can see she cares about you," he says with a soft smile.

I search his eyes. Up close, there's a ring of darker blue surrounding the blue-flecked-with-gold of his irises. I'd almost thought they had to be contacts, but now I can see Theo's 100% pure, natural, probably organic gorgeousness.

I bite my lip. "Are you here to take advantage of me, Theo?"

His eyebrows fly up. "What?"

I turn so I'm facing him more fully. My knees brush against the steel of his thigh in those perfect-fit jeans. "If you're going to take advantage of me, I say, let's do it right now. Right here on the couch. I haven't fucked anyone here yet—kind of kept the couch as a sanctuary, now that I think about it—but for you, I'll make an exception."

He's just blinking at me. "I... don't know what to say to that." He's even more adorable when he's stunned.

I touch his cheek, which makes his eyes go even wider. "You rescued me. You're hot. You're here. Some heavy fucking could be just what I need."

He blinks again then frowns. "Do you..." He leans away from my touch. "Do you really think I would do that? Grace, you're *hurt.*" But by his tone, I can tell *he's* the one who's hurt.

I pull back. "Oh, God." I swallow the sudden dryness in my throat. "I've offended you." The abyss mocks me where it waits, lurking just off the couch. I squeeze my eyes shut, but it doesn't go away, a deep, dark pit that wants to pull me in. "Why can't I do anything right?"

It's not really a question, but Theo answers. "You didn't offend me."

I open my eyes. "Theo, I'm sorry." I give him my most sincere eye apology, then drop my gaze, because *fuck*, I suck at literally everything.

"Hey." His voice is so soft, but then he lifts my chin with a single finger, and that's even softer. And hot. *So hot.* I'm gazing into his eyes now, and he doesn't look hurt anymore. "You're a beautiful woman. *Insanely* beautiful. I'm not even sure I could properly make love to you because I'd be too busy worshipping you like a goddess."

Holy shit. My mouth is hanging open. *So sexy, Grace.* I shut it.

He doesn't seem to notice—too busy flaying my soul with his piercing gaze and hot words. "It would be special, Grace, being with you. Something that would change me forever. That's not the kind of thing I'd take lightly. Or rush into. I would take my time, getting there and staying there and fulfilling every fantasy I'd ever had. I'd figure out yours, too. All of them. And create new ones together. That's not the kind of thing you do with a woman who's hurting. That's something you wait for." He holds me prisoner with those eyes a moment longer then suddenly breaks that contact, dropping his gaze. He laughs a little. "Okay, that was… a pretty weird thing to say out loud."

The flaming heat all over my skin begs to differ. "You *really* should consider acting."

He gives me the cutest, scrunched up look. "I was being serious."

"I *know.*" I fan myself, and I'm not even kidding. "And *damn.* You and words have a hot thing going." Then it clicks. No one grows up dreaming of being a Production Assistant. They're all trying to get into the industry to be one of three things. And if he's not an actor, then it's a director or... "You're a writer."

A smile slowly grows on his face. "Because I was trying to seduce you with words?"

"Because you use words like they're meant to obey you."

He looks shocked again like I haven't said something obvious. I leave out that I would have jumped his hot body even without the sexy brain, but *damn.* And sweet, too? Theo's the whole package. Which of course means he'll want nothing to do with someone fucked up five ways to Sunday like me.

Theo recovers from his shock and drops his gaze. "Grace, I'm not going to—"

I stop him with a hand on his. "I know." Can he feel how heated my skin is? That would be embarrassing. "You're unbelievably sweet and hot. And you're here to take care of me. Which is so... *nice*... I can barely stand it. Where did you come from? Are there more like you on Planet Sweet Stuff? Wait..."

He's still kind of bewildered. "What?"

"If you're a writer, you must have written stuff. Scripts?"

"No, I just write—"

"Novels?"

"I guess you could call it that but—"

"I want to read it."

"What?" He leans away. "No one reads it. It's just for me."

"How can you be a writer if you don't let people read your stuff?" His eyes are getting big, but a surge of excitement makes me blabber on. Because I could help Theo with this—I know people. My folks are crazy connected. We could get his work read by someone. Maybe? I've always focused on the acting side of things. *Silly little Grace who's self-centered and doesn't bother to know things that aren't important to her.* My therapist would cringe at that self-talk, but it's true. I have no idea how you get a novel published. "You have to take risks. Get your work out there in the world." This much I know is true.

He's slowly shaking his head, but it's not really a *no*.

"What?" I give his arm a gentle squeeze. "You've got talent, Theo. I'm sure of it."

"I've never met anyone like you." He says it in a dazed way.

"Okay. Not sure that's a compliment, but…" I nod. "Fair enough."

Slowly, the smile comes back to his face. He really *is* from Planet Sweet Stuff. And he hasn't even questioned this crazy I just put him through. Having someone like him swoop into my life just when I'm melting down… that's the Universe giving me a little help right when I need it. And I haven't had a break like that in a long time.

I retract my hand from his arm and try not to crowd his space so much. "You haven't even asked," I say, not quite able to look in those eyes that are smiling at me. "Why I freaked out so bad."

I peer up. His face has gone solemn. "I just wanted to make sure you were okay."

I let out a sigh. "The director is *so* going to blackball me."

"You're not thinking of going back, are you?" His concern rachets up fast.

"To the set? Acting? Not sure what the point

would be." I grimace as the abyss widens, beckoning me to jump right in. *Not today, black hole of despair!* I've got a hottie on my couch, and he's already dealt with enough from me. But the truth has to be faced. "I've never been very good. As an actor, I mean. Which is fine, I guess." I shrug with one shoulder because acting was always just something I did—it was like breathing. "Putting on a character and a costume, bringing stories and people to life… it's just how I am in the world. It seemed natural to try to make a career out of it. And I *am* a working actor. I get parts." I flick a look at him, feeling defensive, but Theo's attention is too intense, so I go back to picking at stray couch fibers. "I just never landed anything I could really hold up and say, *Look, Mom and Dad! I made it!*"

"Is that important?" His voice is so gentle, I don't feel the wicked cut of the words quite so sharp.

But I do look him in the eyes again. "It didn't used to be. Before my sister, Mari, died, she carried the Successful Sister banner. My dad's, like, this famous architect, and she was carrying on the family tradition, working in his firm, designing new works together. My mom is huge in the art world with her sculptures, and Mari did art, too. Photography. She and Mom were working on an exhibit of arts and crafts and photos, all showcasing the creativity that survived in the internment camps."

Theo lifts his eyebrows.

"I'm half-Japanese," I explain, which is somewhat obvious just looking at me, but people are surprisingly clueless. "Fifth-generation. My father is *yonsei,* fourth generation. His grandparents met in the camps. My great-grandmother was a sculptor, and my great-grandfather was a photographer. Their artistic sensibilities were developed there. A lot of the design work that came after the war was influenced by those in the camps, including my father's architectural career. Mari and Mom were putting together an exhibit for the 75th anniversary of the release from the camps. It's coming up." I pause because a spot in the center of my chest is aching. I try to rub it away.

"That's kind of amazing." Theo's voice is soft, but the way he's peering at me, concerned, helps the pain radiate away.

"That's Mari. *Amazing.*" I smile brightly, but it hurts. "Everything she did was pure gold. I wasn't even jealous." Again, I shrug just one shoulder. It's starting to stiffen. Every muscle in my body feels tight like the panic attack is just now being felt in the soreness everywhere. "Mari was the star, and I was free to be a silly and frivolous actor doing bit parts here and there. I didn't have to be important because *she* was. And then she died." I rush out those last words. I haven't talked about Mari for so long. And I do *not* want to get into how she died. Theo doesn't need to deal with all that.

"How long ago?" His hand finds mine, and it's just warm—not sexy or tantalizing, just comforting.

"Two years." I find his pretty eyes again. "And two months. Eighteen days, I think. I'm honestly not that weird about it. Mostly." I totally am, but I already feel like my chest is about to crack open, exposing all my flaws to this poor guy. I pull in a breath. "Mom never finished the exhibit. I think it's still sitting in her gallery here in Chelsea. For two years, I've been buckling down, *trying* to get serious about my career. Trying to fill that Mari-sized hole in our family. Like, maybe, if I could just make something happen—land a real part, be in a successful series, something—then Mom and Dad would have something to be proud of again. I can't carry on the family business. The only art I've ever managed were these crazy origami animals I made with Mari. All I can really do is act and now…" I shrug, both shoulders this time, and the tears are finally starting to come. "Now I've screwed that up, too. All because I couldn't…" I blink, fast, pulling it back in. Because I can't talk about *that*—not with this sweet guy looking at me like his heart's going to break. *Guess what, Theo? I was abducted by aliens and tortured, and that's why I can't do a hospital scene without losing my shit.* "I couldn't keep it together on set. The pressure was just too much, I guess. And now I've fucked up everything."

Theo brings me in for a hug. A real, honest-to-gosh, wholesome hug, and I simply melt. Like complete goo, just molding against his chest like I've lost all skeletal mass, and now I'm a lump of soggy, sniffling girl. I give silent thanks to the Universe for sending me this crafted-from-steel chest to rest against at this moment in time. I could never have arranged to have someone like Theo in my life without some divine assistance. I can put on any character, play any scene, but I'm really no good with people. There have been guys here and there and a few sort-of girlfriends, but Mari was the sun and the moon and all the planets. My only real best friend. Jayda and even Daisy are sister-friends now, because of what we went through, but I've never felt this comfortable with a guy.

It feels… impossibly good.

I have this weird feeling Theo's on loan from the Universe for a short time, so I should enjoy it while it lasts. Which I do, probably too much as he's stroking my back. Everywhere he touches releases tension. I'm becoming ever-more goo-like. When he finally pulls back a little, I'm almost woozy. I blink at him, trying to focus.

"You sure you're not Human Prozac?" I say, still blinking.

His smile is like the sun heating my face. "I was trying to think of words that might make this better, but maybe my superpower is in being a sedative."

I'm craving his touch again, but not in a sexual way. I realize with a weird jolt that I haven't had anyone to cuddle in literally years. Mari and I would get a faux fur blanket and snuggle for our binge sessions. Since then, the only *touch* I've had…

I jolt again because I don't want to remember what they—the aliens, monsters, whatever they were—did to me. I'm not even sure it was real. And that's the worst feeling. Like I'm *really* having a mental break and maybe all of it was something I made up in my head because losing Mari just broke something inside me and now I'm just… *lost.*

"Grace?" Theo's face is all squished again.

I swallow. "Can we skip the pep talk? Maybe just watch a movie or something?"

"Of course." But his scowl stays etched on his face.

I reach in the back of my corner to flip up the secret compartment with the remote. Theo's eyes go wide as the screen scrolls down from the ceiling.

"Pretty cool, huh?" I hesitate then decide the Universe sent Theo for a reason, and that reason was to be a snuggle partner. There's no sense in being shy about it. I lift his arm and scoot under it, draping it over my shoulders as I bring up Netflix.

He's arching an eyebrow but letting me cuddle up against his broad chest. "We're not doing Netflix and chill, are we?"

"Nope." We'll have to get a blanket and popcorn later. After I've gotten my snuggle fix. "Mari and I used to binge an entire season at once. Marathon session. Breaks only for bathroom and food. Think you can step up, pretty boy? That's a big spot to fill there on the couch." I give his luscious body a thorough eye-scrub like I'm seriously evaluating if he's worthy of sitting there.

He rains that gorgeous smile on me. It's the kind that would give me an instant lady boner and make me *down to fuck* in no time. Except Theo is now squarely in my Cuddle Category, a newly formed designation, just for him, of hot men who are saints. Men Who Are Worthy of Sharing My Sacred Netflix Space, Population: 1.

"The new Star Trek series?" he asks.

"Do you even watch Netflix? That's on HBO or some shit. We're talking *The Chilling Adventures of Sabrina*, the kickass witch."

"*Witch?*" He practically chokes on the word.

"Don't give me shit about it being a teen drama for girls. I will go Full Metal Feminist on you."

"I... wouldn't dream of it." But he looks confused and slightly panicky, which is making me laugh.

"Relax. I won't bite. Hard." Then I snuggle into him and focus on the screen, queueing up the show. As I do, Theo scoots a little, but just to get in a more cuddle-able position, pulling me closer, like he knows he's a safe harbor in the storm of my life, and he wants to make sure I'm properly docked. A warmish glow fills me like I've won the couch-mate lottery. Before the show even gets through the credits, I'm melting into him again.

I have no idea how this is possible. I'm not about to question the Universe, though.

Halfway through the second episode, we break

for popcorn and blankets—two, layered one on top of the other. We're *super* snuggled now. We make it through Episode Four before peeing becomes necessary. Then we're hunkered for the duration.

My eyes are bleary. My body aches from the muscle seizure during the panic attack.

But my heart… my heart is impossibly full.

FOUR

Theo

GRACE MOVES AND PULLS ME OUT OF A DREAM.

I suck in a breath, eyes closed, not moving while I savor the feel of her body tucked against mine on the couch. The dream lingers. I was in that Irish field with the witch who paired us, except in my dream, it was the TV witch, Sabrina. She touched my forehead and summoned the magic that revealed my soul mate. The stunned feeling when I first saw Grace in my mind's eye—beautiful and tormented—still hangs over me, a sharp contrast to the infinite warmth of her body stretched against the length of mine.

She moves again, something making her whimper. And not in a good way.

I open my eyes and lean over to check. Her eyes

are still shut, but they're moving under her lids. Earlier, she changed into comfy yoga pants and a t-shirt, and the Wonder Woman bandaid on her forehead has been replaced with a neutral one, so it doesn't stand out. But there's still bruising all around it. We drifted off before the end of the season, and her show is still running. It's dark out, and our nap has carried us into the evening. I'm not even sure how late it is. I lift the remote from under her hand and switch off the TV. A blanket of silence falls in Grace's super upscale apartment. She twitches next to me, and this time her whimper isn't so soft.

"Grace." I jostle her, hoping that will rouse her, but she just cries a little and curls her hand up against her chest. *"Grace,"* I try again. She's trapped in some nightmare, her body trembling. I work my arm under her, trying to turn her toward me. She gasps, and her eyes fly open. Suddenly, she's a wild thing in my arms, crying out and pushing away. She nearly falls off the couch, but I pull her back from the edge. "It's just a dream. *Grace!*" She freezes, twisting to see me, eyes wide, chest heaving. Then she bursts into tears. "It's okay," I say, bringing her in for a hug. She turns into it and buries her face in my neck. Her arm works up to wrap around my neck. She's *sobbing.* "It's all right." I stroke her head. The hot wetness of her tears reaches my skin.

"They were coming for me." Her words are gasps.

"No one's coming." My heart is breaking. "I've got you."

"I couldn't..." She's trembling in my arms. *"They had me, Theo."* She's still crying.

"No one's going to hurt you," I vow. "I'll keep you safe. I promise." The words calm her. She leans her body a little more into mine. As she sniffles against me, I know this is a vow I can keep. The Vardigah—the bastard elves who hurt her in the first place—can't find her again. They don't have the witch to guide them anymore. But they're alive inside Grace's head, and I'll do whatever it takes to kill the memory of them so it can't torment her. The moment I saw her face in my mind for the first time, when Alice paired us, I knew I would do anything to keep her safe. But spending all day on the couch, snuggling and talking, eating popcorn and laughing... she's showing me the real Grace. The one inside the snark and the sexual propositions. The part that's grieving her sister and terrified of the Vardigah, even though she hasn't admitted that part yet. This Grace feels all alone in the world.

I'm supposed to be seducing her, but that's not what she *needs*. She needs someone to hold her and protect her—not from the elves, but from the damage they've done. And I'm powerless to say no to that. I'm not in love with Grace Tanaka. But I will fucking kill anything that hurts her… including the memories she has in her head.

She pulls back, eyes red and wet.

I hold her cheek. "I will beat the shit out of anything that tries to hurt you," I vow again. We're close, nose to nose, lying side-by-side on the couch. She's beautiful and broken, and my heart hurts seeing the fear still on her face.

"You can't…" Her lips tremble, and she shudders in my arms. "This isn't something you can punch, Theo."

The dreams? The Vardigah? Are we finally going to talk about what really happened? "You might be surprised what I can fight. But trust me— nothing's going to hurt you on my watch." If somehow the Vardigah *did* show up, they'd be eating my razor-sharp talons in a heartbeat.

Her eyes go a little wide, and a sigh escapes her. "You mean that."

"Yeah." I don't have to lean forward much to boop her nose with mine. "I do."

Her eyes search mine. The fear is gone, replaced by wonder. She drops her gaze, and suddenly, her lips press against mine. Her arms tighten around me. I don't expect it, don't know what to do with it, but she's moving her entire body against mine, lips trying to devour mine, and suddenly, something in me roars to life. I cup the back of her head and open my mouth, plundering hers with my tongue without preamble, without invitation. Her whimper this time lights me on fire. I grab her arm from around my neck and stretch it overhead, then I tuck her under me, my full weight pressing her slender, delicious body into the couch. My hands pin hers above her head, against the cushion. My body is claiming hers with our clothes on. My heart cracks wide open, and I weld to her, body and soul. She's writhing under me, but she can barely move.

It's a True Kiss. The magic of it shoots like lightning through my body, hot and electric. Somewhere in the depths of my brain, something screams, *Stop!* Because what the fuck am I doing? *This isn't the plan, Theo.*

I yank back from the kiss, breathing hard. Grace couldn't look more shocked.

"I'm sorry," I gasp. I've got her pinned to the couch like a fucking Neanderthal. I try to move off her, but she's so completely under me, and I don't want to hurt her—I end up half-rolling, half-stumbling off the couch. She barely props herself up, mouth agape, her body still laid flat. I rub my hand across my face. *What the fuck, Theo.* "I'm so sorry—"

"Theo."

I bunch up my fist and press it to my head. "I shouldn't have—"

"Theo!" She's telling me to shut up, so I do. "That kiss was… no one's ever kissed me like that."

I can't even begin to speak.

"Grace?"

I whip around so fast, I nearly fall. Jayda's standing on the threshold to the entryway, murder on her face.

"Are you all right?" She's talking to Grace as she strides fast across the room.

I wipe the look of shock off my face. *Did she see us grappling on the couch?* Fuck. I scramble to put innocence on my face, but it's impossible. Instead, I just back away from the couch, giving them tons of room.

"I'm fine." Grace is waving her off, but she's a mess. Hair mussed from sleep. Tears and redness still in her eyes from crying. *From the dream,* not me, but Jayda doesn't know that.

Jayda takes a seat on the couch next to her. Grace is gathering the furry blanket up like a protective shield. She's not talking, just retreating into the cocoon we've spent the day building together. Only I'm no longer there. It looks bad. Really bad.

Jayda's glare in my direction is full of deadly promise. "You can go now. I'll be here *all night* with Grace." It's a warning.

"Theo?" Grace's still-teary eyes find mine across half the room. "You're coming back in the morning, right?"

Jayda whips her head to Grace. "If you need someone, honey... I can take tomorrow off." She's resolute.

Grace shakes her head. "You need to work."

"You don't need *Theo* as a babysitter." Jayda's tone is all business and rationality now. But I still hear the deadly threat underneath. "I can find someone else to stay with you, maybe a nurse with some medical background? Or just a nurse's aide, if you simply don't want to be alone—"

"I'll be here if you want me," I say. That earns a hostile look from Jayda, but she doesn't get to decide, no matter what she thinks of me. Grace does.

She grabs Jayda's hand and holds it to her chest. "Theo's not a babysitter. He's my friend." When she seems unimpressed, Grace quickly adds, "And he's my protector."

Jayda's expression opens up. "Oh, honey…" She visibly swallows. "You're *safe* now. We're…" She stops herself, glances at me again, then drops her voice to nearly a whisper. "We're *all* safe now. I promise."

Grace looks her deep in the eyes. "You don't know that."

"I *do,*" Jayda says, emphatically. "I swear it." She gives me a more pointed look of disgust this time. "We can talk about this tonight." She means after I leave.

Which is fine… as long as Grace lets me come back. As much as I wish there was a way to write myself out of this story, I can't—Grace needs me, and only one thing could keep me away. Grace herself.

I look to her and wait.

She squeezes Jayda's hand with both of hers. "I don't need a nurse." She looks at me. "I need a bodyguard."

Jayda's eyes fly open. "A bodyguard—what has he been *saying* to you—"

"I can do that." I smile from across the room, and Grace returns it.

Jayda is still sputtering, but it doesn't matter. That's all I needed. "I'll see you in the morning."

Grace's eyes light up.

I turn to leave.

"Grace, honey, you don't need…" Jayda's voice fades as I leave the apartment.

On the way out, I pass the overnight bag Jayda brought. She really is planning to stay all night. Grace had given her the code for the door earlier. I remember it, but if Jayda has anything to do with it, the code will be changed before I come back in the morning. I have Grace's number, too, so that won't keep me out. Not if Grace wants me in.

I'm a mess as I ride the elevator down.

That kiss. Holy magic. I've heard the stories all my life. The fairy tale of how soul mates, when they meet, they share a True Kiss, and their hearts are opened to one another. Falling in love after that is supposedly as natural as breathing. And when they mate, the sex is incredible. Okay, that part wasn't in the fairy tale my parents told me—that's the scoop I got from the other young and horny dragons, all fucking their way through the female population that Niko, the Lord of the North Lair, kept circulating through the main house. All my cousins and brothers and friends—the legendary sex that awaited us as mated dragons was the nirvana that kept us going. Sure, we were trying to save the species from dying out and wanted to find our soul mates, our literal other halves, but what got everyone dressed up on Friday nights was the idea of the Ultimate Fuck.

It always made me cringe.

Not that I wasn't horny, too. But I have a vivid imagination, and I know how to use my hand. Getting off wasn't an issue. Fucking random women in hopes that one might be your soul mate? That got old after the first dozen. It got excruciating after the first fifty. I'm only twenty-five—I've been part of the circuit since I was eighteen—that's only seven years of that soul-sucking shallowness. I was ready to punch out even then. I have no idea how the dragons who are two hundred years old—the ones from the Old Times—haven't gone out of their damn minds.

And now I'm here, with Grace… *and that kiss.* Maybe I'm wrong. Maybe this mating thing could be the way to go. It twists me up inside because 1) I'm not here to fuck Grace, I'm here to help her heal, but my imagination already has her up against a wall, moaning and coming around my cock. Which makes me an utter bastard. And 2) *I'm not here to mate at all.* I've already decided this. The plan was to make sure Grace was okay—truly all right, healed and healthy and ready to chase after her dreams, whatever they were—*and then leave.* Or rather stay, somewhere in the city. Or maybe go to LA. Wherever I need to be to pursue *my* dreams. I wasn't strictly planning to run away... but if I'm honest, that's what it looks like. Walking away from the commitment. Leaving the lair and my family behind. Abdicating my duty to save the species.

Because fuck all that. I deserve to have a life too.

I was already working up the courage to leave before Alice the Witch showed up. And now... they don't need me anymore! Alice connected literally every dragon over the age of eighteen to his mate. That's a mate for every dragon on earth. Which means we're not in a desperate bid to avoid extinction anymore. Every last dragon need not commit their lives to the endless pursuit of reproduction alone. Not anymore. At least, in theory.

And then... *Grace.* And that kiss.

Now I'm stalking the streets of the city with half a hard-on and confused as hell. It's nighttime. I don't even know how late until I look at my phone.

8pm. Too early to sleep—as if I could, anyway. Morning, when I get to see Grace again, feels like a million hours away. I need to talk to someone about this. The six-hour drive to the North Lair in the Thousand Islands is too far. I should just go back to my apartment and…

Ree. He's my roommate, and more importantly, he's one of the older dragons. And the dude is a fucking stoic. Solid as a rock. Older than dirt. If anyone has insight into this, it'll be him.

I stop stomping down the sidewalk and text him. *Do you have a minute to talk?* I wait. Nothing comes back. I'm stopped outside a Starbucks, so I step inside and order a coffee. We don't have things like this at the lair, and I've quickly become addicted to the city's amenities, including Venti black coffee with two shots espresso and a kiss of milk. Because I will probably be up all night anyway.

Ree's text comes back. Finally. *Kinda busy.*

I groan—loudly—then apologize to the barista who's looking at me like she might need to call the cops. *Need to talk,* I text back. Then, because I need something to get him to agree, *I saw your soul mate.*

Give me five minutes. At the apt.

What? I sip my coffee then head for the train.

It'll take me longer than that to get back to our place in Midtown. Which gives me time to puzzle through why Ree needs time if he's already at the apartment. *Wait, is he…* why would a dragon be fucking around when his soul mate is waiting right here in the city?

My suspicions are confirmed when I cross paths with a hot blonde as I exit the elevator. Her long hair is wet, but she doesn't look frustrated, so Ree must have finished—or rather Ree finished *her*—before he shoved her out the door.

I'm having second thoughts about going to Ree for advice.

I finish the coffee and use my key to open the door. The caffeine is zinging through my body, and I was already amped up by Grace, the kiss, my whole situation. Ree cruises out of his bedroom with a towel around his waist and nothing else. His hair is wet. So they fucked in the shower. Amazing. I'm suddenly glad we don't share one.

He swipes the damp hair out of his face—it's long, the way a lot of the older dragons wear it. He's got the same dark features as those from the original Athens lair, but Ree's actually from the Euro lair—he wears a perpetual five-o'clock shadow. I don't know his background except that he was rogue for a long time, one of those dragons that leaves the lairs and circulates among the human population, giving up on the species. And he's clearly in no hurry to mate. Which, if I'm honest, isn't far different from me. That Ree and I have this in common does *not* make me happy. But maybe he is the right person to talk to after all.

Ree glances at my empty coffee cup. "You didn't bring me one. I'm disappointed in you, Theo."

Fuck you, is a little too ready on my lips. "I wasn't thinking straight," I say instead.

He crosses the living room and steps into the small kitchen. Dragons are good with money, and the North Lair's been around for two hundred years. To say that we're well-capitalized is a vast understatement. Even so, Niko can be on the frugal side, and city rents are crazy high. Our apartment isn't terrible, but it's not exactly vast. Nothing like our apartments up at the lair. And not even in the same zip code as Grace's insanely upscale apartment in Chelsea. That's one thing that's slowed down the Theo Runs Away plan—cash. Supporting myself as a writer in the city is unlikely in the extreme—I'd need something like the PA job Niko landed for me as cover. Figuring out actual employment is a side project I have going while I'm here, supporting Grace until she's on her feet again. My Production Assistant gig might pay enough to get by if I can get something full-time—I'm only a temp on Grace's set. I toss my Starbucks cup in the recycle bin. That's a habit I won't be able to afford once I'm off dragon money.

Ree's Keurig-brewed coffee is done. He crosses his arms, cup in one hand, and leans back against the counter to study me. "You wanted to talk?"

I notice he doesn't lead with his soul mate. So, naturally, I do. "I met Jayda."

His jaw works. He looks down at his coffee, takes a sip, winces.

"She's gorgeous," I offer. Why the fuck hasn't he gone to see her yet? We've been here for a week. And why doesn't he want to talk about her?

His eyes narrow. "You have your own mate. Stay away from mine."

My eyebrows lift. Okay, maybe he *does* care. "Have you made contact yet?"

"Don't see how that's your business."

Okay, then. Three of us—me, Ree, and Akkan— came to the city to look after our mates, once it was determined it was best to return them to the real world outside the lair's hospice. As far as I know, Akkan hasn't spent a single night in the apartment

—his mate's still in the hospital where we dropped her off, and he's always there. Ree, on the other hand, has been here at the apartment the whole time.

Waiting. For something. I don't know what, but why come here at all if he doesn't want to mate? I study the carefully-composed, no-emotion expression he always wears. It's like he's locked up inside four nested steel vaults with an electrified fence and barbed wire strapped across the KEEP OUT sign. Maybe he's got another plan for all this... just like me.

"Look, I don't care what your intentions are," I start. Then I shake my head. "That's a lie—I do care, but not because I want to pry into your business. That's between you and your mate."

"She's not my mate." He takes another wincing sip of coffee.

"Your *other half.* Soul mate. Whatever." I put my hands up in surrender. "I thought maybe you could help me with *mine*—I don't know what I'm doing with Grace—but, you know what? Never mind." I give an unimpressed glance at the towel around his waist. "You've got your own things going on." I turn my back on him before I say something that'll lead to blows.

I'm halfway to my room when I hear him say, "Kid."

I stop and turn back. "What?"

He steps out of the kitchen. "You don't want advice from me. I don't have anything good to give you. Talk to Niko. He's mated. He's the Lord of your lair. He'll have better advice for you than I ever will." Then he turns and walks with his coffee back to his room.

Whatever Ree's problem is, I have a feeling, it's darker than mine. And also not mine to solve.

I pull out my phone and text Niko. *I've got a problem. Skype?* Then I head into my room in search of fresh clothes. As soon as I change out of my PA shirt, Niko texts back. *Be there in a second.*

What? Just as I realize I haven't thought this through *at all,* Niko appears by my side.

"Shit!" I jump half a foot. Fucking mated dragons and their teleporting.

Niko's eyebrows hike up. "I told you I was coming."

"Yeah, but—"

He steps forward and clasps a hand on my shoulder. "Let's go somewhere more private."

Before I can reply, he's teleported us back to his study. I've been in it a dozen times, so I recognize it immediately—tall bookshelves, ostentatious carved-wood desk—and suddenly, I feel like this was all a terrible, terrible idea.

"What's on your mind, Theo?" Niko folds his arms and leans back against his desk. He's from the original Athen's lair—an older dragon, mated, leader for two hundred years of survival of our kind at the edge of extinction—and I'm going to what? Tell him I want to punch out?

"I… I made contact with my mate."

He smirks. "That doesn't sound like a problem."

I turn to the window and run a hand through my hair. The moon is out, lighting up the familiar world of lakes and trees and castles I grew up with. *This is home.* My people. My family. Am I really going to turn my back on all of it?

Niko comes up next to me, peering out the window, too. "You can't be homesick already." He lifts an eyebrow. "But if you are, you can bring her here. Grace, right?"

I nod. Then I notice the dark circles under Niko's eyes. "You okay?"

"Me?" He cracks a grin. "Yeah, just a little tired. You're not the only dragon having *problems,* Theo. Whatever it is, trust me, I've already heard it."

"Really?" Everything in me sits up and takes notice. "What kind of problems?"

He rests against the window sill and counts them off on his fingers. "Can't get a first date with their mates. Can't get a *second* date. Showing their dragons too early. Not showing their dragons at all. I swear to all that's magic, it's like they've forgotten everything they know about romancing women despite doing it for decades or, in some cases, *hundreds* of years."

I blow out a breath. At least I'm not fucking up like that. "It's the stakes."

"Sorry?"

"The stakes are higher now." I was so mired in my own personal drama—my own perspective—I hadn't thought about everyone else. "Young or old. Experienced or not. It's not just romancing some girl with a million-in-one shot of being your mate. This is The One. You've got to get it right, or you're waiting another lifetime for your second chance to come around. If you're lucky. The older ones have to be *really* stressed. They don't have a spare lifetime hanging around."

Niko smirks. "You want to come work for me? I need a part-time therapist to help these knuckleheads."

I half-laugh, but it's not even funny, so I just grimace at the moon. "I'm not the right person to give other people advice." *Fuck,* now I sound like Ree.

Niko's expression falls serious. "Tell me the trouble with Grace."

"It's not Grace." I give him a sideways glance, but it just feels guilty. "It's me." I rub my forehead, trying to push away the headache rushing across it. Time to step up. I turn and face Niko fully. "What if I'm not ready to mate?"

He cocks his head like he's not sure if I'm joking. "Oh, trust me, you'll be *ready* when the time comes."

I cringe.

Niko leans back. "You're serious. You don't *want* to mate." It's like I've proclaimed I don't *want* to breathe. "I don't understand. Do you not feel the pairing bond?"

"Yeah, I do."

His eyebrows lift. "Is she just not attractive to you?" This concerns him even more—like he thinks there's something physically wrong with me. Or maybe my brain is broken.

"No, that's just it." I fold my arms across my chest, feeling bound up in every way with this.

"She's incredible. Beautiful. Funny. Sweet in a way I don't think she even realizes. I'm worried about her. Protective of her. I'd fucking kill anything that hurt her. And I just spent an entire day snuggling on the couch with her, and all I can think about is…" I swallow. "I want her in my bed like I've wanted no other woman."

"I fail to see the problem here." Niko's expression would be comical if it weren't so exasperating.

I throw my hands out. "I *know* where this is going. And I don't want to get in too deep when I'm just going to leave!"

It's like I've smacked him in the face. He's not hurt—just stunned. "Leave? Where would you go?"

I put both hands in my hair this time and pull like I'm going to rip it out. Then I drop my hands, turn back to the window, and sigh. "I have no idea. I just know I'm not ready to mate and make baby dragons and carry on the dragon race." And that's not even it, but I can't bring myself to say, *I want to pursue my writing.* Because it sounds childish. And even that's an excuse. The truth is that I'm chafing under a lifetime of expectations, and I just want to be *free.* Free to make my own decisions. The designer of my own destiny. Not have to follow the dictates of fate just because that's how it's always been for my people.

"Theo." Niko's dropped his voice and placed his hand on my shoulder. "I promise you—mating's not a burden."

"Yeah, I'm sure it's amazing." I turn to face him. "That's what I'm worried about."

He frowns like he still doesn't understand. And I don't know why I expected he might. "Maybe I'm not the right person to talk to about this," he says. "Have you checked in with your folks? I'm sure Vasil would have some advice—"

I cut that off with a wave before he can get too far. "They're busy with the baby." My mother and father are already onto their *second* batch of kids, doing their duty for the dragon race. They waited until the first batch—me and my two older brothers —was grown, but repopulating the dying dragon species is a big thing with my father. Which I get. He has his own tragic backstory. But he's *not* the person to talk to about this.

Niko's looking more concerned. "What about your brothers? I hear they're both in Europe now."

No doubt romancing their newly-found soul mates, like they're supposed to. They've always been eager for the Friday night seduction grind, cheered on by our father, so I'm sure they're hot after their soul mates now. Even my mother was a huge fan of the whole racket.

I was always odd-dragon-out in my own family.

"I shouldn't distract them." I force a smile. "I've probably just got cold feet. It'll be fine. Just need a little time to sort it out." I sigh because I can't sustain the smile. "Can we go back now?"

"Sure." His hand's already on my shoulder, so an instant later, we've teleported back to my room. He releases me and steps back. "If you need to come home for a while, Theo, that would be okay."

Great. He thinks this is some childish thing I'll get over. Or that I'm homesick. I plaster the smile back on. "Thanks. But I'm good. Just need some time to make it work."

He's still frowning when he teleports away.

Fuck. I stare at my bed, thinking I should just crash, but my imagination puts Grace in it, squirming underneath me while I devour her with my mouth. I take out my phone, halfway to texting her, but then I realize Jayda's there, probably trying to talk her out of having me return in the morning. My mind races ahead to tomorrow. Jayda's gone back to work. It's just Grace and me in her apartment. That magical connection between us makes every touch, every kiss, insanely hot. We've got *all day* to explore what we can do with that.

My cock is there already.

There's only one thing for me to do about that.

I pull off the new shirt I just put on, tossing it on the bed as I head to the shower. My bathroom is right off the bedroom, the white-and-gray décor spare and functional. I turn on the water, quickly filling the room with steam as I peel off the rest of my clothes. I push past the curtain and step in, the water just right to heat my skin and ward off the chill of the air. I brace my hand against the wall, a little soap to make things move well, and I take my cock in hand. I'm already hard as a rock, but when I close my eyes and see Grace, her clothes long gone, her eyes wide with excitement, it's like I'm stroking a steel bar. I pin her up against a wall, hands flat, and I take her from behind, each stroke so hard, I jolt a whimper out of her. She's up on her toes, cute little bottom pushing back into me, braced for the pounding I'm meting out. I stroke harder, and I know it's just my own hand, but *fuck*, I can feel her coming around me... and suddenly, I'm releasing in the shower, coming hard and gushing so long, pulsing and pulsing... I stroke the whole thing out, until every last twitch fades, and I'm soft again.

I rest my forehead against my hand braced on the tile. I'm fucking *panting.* I haven't come that hard in... I don't know how long. And that's just Fantasy Grace.

Real Grace will kill me.

Niko is right. There's no way I'll be able to resist her. No way I won't want the mating with every fiber of my being. I can already feel it building again, the need for her. The images of her. Before I can force myself out of the shower, my cock is back at full strength, demanding attention.

I am so fucked.

I groan my way through beating off again, then slap off the water and stomp out of the shower, not caring what gets wet.

I have to get out now. Before it's too late.

FIVE

Grace

JAYDA SLEPT ON THE COUCH AND WAS UP BEFORE dawn.

I texted Theo the second she left for work. *Door's unlocked. Bring snacks.*

He hasn't replied.

I put the final folds on another paper crane and coax it into shape—wings extended, ready to take flight, beak turned down, tail pointed high. I've been making them for two years, ever since that day I found out about Mari. Strangely enough, she and I never made cranes together. Hippos and lions, dogs and deer, yes. One year, we even made a pangolin—well, Mari did. Mine looked more like an armadillo that went through the paper shredder. But Mari never met a challenge she didn't like, and hers was truly a work of art. I was happy to do whatever, as long as it was our thing.

I set the finished crane next to the other five I've made, waiting for Theo to text back. I peek at my phone. Still nothing. I slide over another perfect square of paper and start again. I had to beg Jayda to go out for papercraft at ten o'clock last night. Only SoHo had a place open with the right supplies. I wanted to fold when we got home, but she insisted we go to bed.

I knew I wouldn't be sleeping much, especially after that nightmare I had on the couch. Which brings my thoughts back to Theo... *and that insane kiss.* I thought maybe I wasn't his type. Or that all the cuddling had been just *too* sweet. Or perhaps Theo was simply the real deal, a true friend, being a cuddle bear because I needed that most... and that all the lusty thoughts were strictly on my side of the blanket.

But no. That was no casual kiss. I've never felt so much *want* in the form of bodily contact before—and I've done a few things that were definitely on the sexually adventurous side. With people *serious* about their kinks. I'm a mostly vanilla girl, but I'm up for a little weirdness on any given day and doubly so if it involves orgasms. *But Theo...* that wasn't some boner-driven pawing on the couch. He *desired* me, every part of me, every *inch* of me—and I felt it drill straight into my soul, cracking me open and leaving me emotionally naked, ready for whatever ravishing he intended. My mind literally blanks out when thinking about sex with Theo. Like... I can't even get past the hotness of that kiss. It makes me shiver and come alive in a way I thought maybe had died when I lost Mari.

The desire to live again.

Theo woke that up in me.

Which makes it maddening as fuck that he hasn't texted me back. Is he sleeping? It's only eight, but Jayda left hours ago.

I cave and text him again. *Hey, sleepyhead. Don't worry about snacks. Just come over when you're up.* Stalkerish? Needy? I decide it's okay and send it.

I go back to folding cranes. I'd fallen off making them for a while. They stay here in the second bedroom, the one Mari would sleep in. The table where I work sits under an elaborate brass lamp Mari found somewhere. She'd come and stay the weekend, getting away from the bustle of the office and her life with Mom and Dad. She always had a hundred gigawatts of energy powering her through. This was our quiet time. Our getaway.

My phone buzzes, and I practically mangle the crane in my haste to check it.

It's not Theo. *It's my mom.*

"What?" I screech out loud.

The text says, *I'm at the door, let me in.*

Holy shit. I scramble up from my chair, hesitate, thinking I should hide everything, but that's crazy— I'll just shut the door. I scuttle out of Mari's room, pulling the door closed, and race to the front door. Before I can get there, Mom's already knocking rapid-fire like a crazy person.

I yank open the door. "Mom! You're… here." My brain is throwing fits, trying to figure out *why.* She's literally never been here. I'm kind of shocked she knows where it is. But of course, she does—she and Dad pay the rent.

"Grace! You're all right." She scoops me up in a hug I barely think to return before she pulls back. Then she quickly finds the band-aid on my head— it's hardly visible, but my visual-arts mother doesn't miss a thing. Plus there's the bruising. "You're hurt!" she declares like she's just discovered my skull cracked wide open.

"It's just a scratch. Mom, why are you even here?" It's a little too blunt, and I regret it immediately, but I am expecting Theo any moment, and that would be highly awkward. And something I do not want to explain to my mother.

She sighs—deeply—and gives me a ponderous look.

My mother is dramatic—I definitely got my drama llama from her, not my soft-spoken father—but she never gets truly mad at anyone except politicians who cut funding for the arts. Those she'd put in a pillory in Times Square if she could. No, her expression is more concerned, with soft lines around her deep brown eyes, and her exquisitely pale skin pulled tight into a frown. She has a regal bearing about her—I think there's some French nobility among her ancestors. I look more like a female version of my father—the Japanese genes are strong—but on my better days, I have about half the razor-sharp fashion sense my mom carries like a birthright. She can pull off literally anything. Today she's decked out in an oversized, black coat-dress that hides her slender frame. It wraps around like she might step out into Central Park and flash someone, but the clunky platform boots are straight out of a teen goth's closet. Her iconic, oversized sunglasses are pushed up on her head, holding back her silver-streaked black bob. Massive wide silver hoops hanging from her ears complete the look.

"I went to the set," she says, still holding onto my shoulders as she examines my band-aid-covered head wound. "They said you were hurt yesterday, and they had to call an ambulance." Her scowl finds my face. *"Yesterday,* Grace! Why didn't you tell us?"

I wish I had now. "I'm sorry. I've just been resting." Belatedly, I move out of the doorway, so she can come in. Which she does, but she's not done examining me, so we stay in the foyer.

"What *happened?* And are you sure you're okay? Have you been to the doctor? You need to have that horrible looking bruise on your head checked out. We can take you into the ER if you can't get an appointment. These doctors are too busy. It's ridiculous—"

"Mom." I slip my hands into hers because now they're fluttering all around my body, which is a thing she does when she has too much energy and nowhere to put it. "I'm okay. The paramedics said I didn't have a concussion. Friends brought me home. I had one stay here with me last night. I'm really okay."

She purses her lips, but her hands aren't jittery anymore. "You're sure."

"I'm sure." I frown. "Why were you even on the set?"

She shrugs in a way that's unnatural. "Can't I just check in on your new show?"

I cock my head to the side. "You've literally never done that before. And I'm not ten, Mom. That's a little weird."

Her sigh is long and drawn out this time.

My heart sinks. "Is something wrong? Is Dad okay?"

She waves that off. "Oh, no, your father's fine. Not that I ever see him. He's always at the office." She peeks down the hallway toward the rest of the apartment. Even though she insisted on having her famous friends do the interior design of the place, and she personally arranged for her sculpture to be delivered as a house-warming gift, she's never actually been here. At first, she was just too busy with Mari and the exhibit. Then Mari was gone… and everything just kind of fell apart.

"Come on in," I offer, lamely.

She steps into the living room and gives it an approving nod. I send up a small prayer of thanks for that—and the fact that I tidied up during one of my manic bouts of insomnia last night.

When she turns back, she takes her glasses off her head, folds them carefully, and tucks them in an invisible pocket in her voluminous coat-dress. "Grace."

"Yeah?" Something's wrong.

Her tight smile just strings tension in my shoulders. "I *did* come down to see your show. And I'm glad you're okay. I should have texted or called, I simply didn't think and had to race over to make sure…" She blinks a little too much and looks away.

I swallow a giant lump in my throat. "I'm sorry I worried you."

She turns back and puts a warm hand to my cheek. "You've always been easy, Grace. I never had to worry about you. Until you disappeared for two weeks without telling us. *Now* I worry. Don't do that again, okay? I just can't have anything happen to you."

"I know." I can barely get the words out.

She pulls me into another hug, this one long and the kind I always melted into as a kid. Dad's a hugger, too, under the right circumstances, but Mom was always the one who held us for as long as we needed, enough for the tears and sniffles to stop. This is why I can't tell them anything about what happened. Why my mom and dad think I was out of town with my "new friends" Jayda and Daisy, going on a spontaneous road trip across the country. Why I said I got the flu, and we had to come home early. That explained the black eyes and weakness. That let me sequester in my apartment, locking the door from the inside for days until I recovered enough to be around people again. Jayda went back to work right away. It was crazy. But I spent two days apologizing via text to my parents for my "thoughtlessness" in disappearing for two weeks. Because I was in another dimension being tortured by aliens. Or I was having a mental break. I honestly don't know anymore.

My mom finally releases me, and we're both glassy-eyed, but the smile on her face is less stressed now. Which is good. Whatever this madness is doing to me, I won't let it affect my parents. They've been through too much already.

She draws in a big breath and lets it out. "I also came down to meet with a buyer for the gallery."

"What?" Alarm trips through me. "But the exhibit—"

"Is never going to be complete." She gives me a look like I'm a child, and she has to explain the ways of the world.

But I'm *not* a child. I just didn't think— "But that's *your* gallery. You've had it since... I don't know… forever. What about your works?" I know they're in storage right now, but…

She gives me a pinched look, drawing herself up and folding her arms across her chest. "I haven't made anything for two years, Grace. I don't know if I ever will again."

The tears surge up, and I can't even worry about them because a panicky feeling in my chest is making it hard to breathe. "You just need time. To get back your flow. Your rhythm."

She shrugs like this is unimportant. But it's *not*. I know it's everything. "The gallery is prime space in Chelsea. Someone should put it to use. If it cannot be me, then someone's living art should be there to enrich the world." My mom's a true believer in the mystical energy that art brings to the Universe. She means every word she's saying. But I know there's far more to this than simply serving the mystical Gods of Art. She wipes the emotion from her face with a pass of her hand. When she looks me in the eyes, I'm still searching for a way to stop this. "I have several offers. I haven't even met them all yet. But the exhibit is a mausoleum, Grace. You have to know this. And I just can't…" She looks away again, tears filling her eyes. "I don't want to look at it anymore."

"Oh, Mom." I want to hug her, but it feels strange. Like she's barely holding it together, and if I touch her, that veneer might shatter.

She turns back, takes my face in her hands, and kisses my bruised forehead. My tears are just gushing now. *How can I fix this?* She sniffs and pulls back, her voice going all business-like. "Once the gallery's gone, I'll be selling my loft in Chelsea as well. I'm never there, anyway, and I want to be home for the few times your father actually decides to leave the office." Her voice softens. "Come home, Grace. Back to Midtown. Your room is still there. We'll get rid of this place and leave Chelsea to the memories we have here."

I'm so surprised, I almost don't know what to say. "But I like it here."

She gives me a pained smile. "I know you like being on your own. And if you want to stay, that's fine. I just... I wanted you to know the offer was open. Your father wants it, too."

That stabs me in the heart. *Dad wants me home.* Like Mari used to be. She always lived with them... right until she moved out with that asshole boyfriend of hers. The one we're sure murdered her, but the police have no evidence, no way to prove it. She was found in the river, strangled, maybe raped, but most of the evidence washed away with the tide. Could have been a random psycho. Or maybe it was the boyfriend who slowly drew her away from her family and jealously controlled her every movement. I know who I'd like to string up. But there's no proof, so we're left with nothing but rage and grief and the giant shattering breakdown of my family that's been happening ever since.

"Well." Mom's trying to pull it together.

I can't stop the tears that keep leaking from my eyes.

"You think about it, sweetie." She gives me a quick hug, but it's distant again. Like she's got to wrap everything up in her dress-coat and keep it all held tight. "I just wanted to let you know about the gallery."

"Okay." *Mari's art.* It's hanging all over the walls. Pictures of the camps. Photos of the internees and their art. Samples of the work they'd done, that she somehow unearthed and mounted on display pedestals next to the original photographs she recovered from our great-grandmother's albums. The subject matter is intense, but that was Mari. Brilliant and intense… and my mom can't look at it anymore.

She gives me one more hug on the way out, making me promise I'll text her later.

I close the door and stagger back to Mari's room. It's filled with the origami we made together. Her bed still made from two years ago. *A mausoleum.* My mom's not wrong, but I don't want to look away. I don't want to *forget* her. I shuffle back to the table, sit down, and fold another crane. And then another. I keep wiping away the tears until they stop coming and keep folding. I don't know how much time passes. My fingers get numb from all the pressing, so I have to take a break. I drag my body to the kitchen, make a bowl of soup, eat it in silence as I squint at the city. I can't see Mom's gallery from here, but it's not far. Two blocks. I could walk there right now. But the cranes are calling me. I leave the dish in the sink and march back. My hands cramp, so I massage them, shake them out, and keep going. The cranes don't fit on the table, so I populate all the horizontal surfaces. The dresser. The shelves where Mari kept her miniature replicas of architectural wonders from around the world. The nightstand that held her phone at night. Finally, I place the cranes on the bed because the only space left is the floor, and I don't want them to get smashed.

My fingers ache. I take a break and stare at the

time. 3pm. I blearily realize Theo never texted back. I massage my fingers into functioning and text him. *Hey, you okay? I could use a bodyguard today. Text me back or I'll call 911 for a wellness check on you.* Not a threat I can follow up on—I literally have no idea where he lives—but concern for him struggles up out of the haze of endless folding. Did he decide I was just too intense after all? Did Jayda track him down and issue some terrifying edict? Or did he fall down an open manhole and was now lying paralyzed somewhere below the streets, waiting for someone to rescue him?

I would totally climb into a sewer for Theo. But it's more likely he's got something better to do than be my "bodyguard." Very reasonable. Except that kiss...

My phone buzzes. *I've got something I need to tell you.*

Oh, shit. *Come over,* I text back. Then I curl up my hands and tap my fists nervously against my mouth. Please, please come. I don't know why it feels so desperate. I pick up my phone again. *Please don't text break up with me,* I type but don't send. Theo and I aren't together—that's a stupid thing to say, even though I feel it with all my bones. I erase that and type, *Door's open.*

Be there in 20, his text comes back, and suddenly, I can breathe again.

Now my hands are super jittery. I shake them out, rub them to warm them up, then fold again. It's crazy. I know that. But it's the only thing keeping me sane right now.

I fold and fold and fold… and wait for Theo to arrive.

SIX

Theo

—————

I ALMOST TURN BACK AT HER DOOR.

In truth, I've nearly punched out three times on the way to Grace's apartment. I was on my way out —literally at Penn Station, getting a train ticket to LA—when I buckled. *I could use a bodyguard today.* What did that mean? Was she okay? The idea that she might *not* be okay, and I was ghosting her, leaving town without explanation... I just couldn't be that guy.

I stand outside her apartment, hand on the doorknob. I should simply check on her and then leave. Or maybe explain that I'm not coming back, and she'll need to call Jayda if she needs help. Or possibly spend one more day with her, make sure she's on her feet, then get the hell out of New York.

I just spent everything I have from the PA gig on the ticket that's burning hot in my jeans pocket. I can change my ticket if I have to. Delay it a day.

Or maybe that's the worst thing I could do.

I'm frozen at her door. *Fuck, Theo, just do it.* I push open the unlocked door and step inside. She's not in the main room. I glance at my phone—with all my dithering, it's taken me almost an hour to get here. She's not in the kitchen, either. My heart rate kicks up a notch. Maybe something's *really* wrong. I hurry down the hall to her bedroom, which I haven't been invited to previously. She's not there. I check the bathroom. Nothing. In a moment of panic, I wonder if I missed her body lying on the floor in the living room. Then I realize there's another bedroom down the hall and the door's open…

I hustle down there but then freeze in the doorway. Grace is hunched over a table, madly focused on folding a piece of paper. There are little origami creatures *everywhere.*

"What is going on here?"

"Ah!" She jumps half a foot and literally falls out of her chair.

I race across the room and scoop her off the floor before I think about what I'm doing. Now she's in my arms, breathing hard, lips parted, and looking up at me like she wants me to close the gap between us.

"Are you okay?" I demand, a little too harshly by the way she shrinks back, but it's taking every restraint I have not to smash my mouth against hers.

"I'm fine." She frowns like maybe I'm crazy.

I slowly release the rock-hard grip I have on her arms and step back. My heart's hammering. I can't look her in the eyes, so I sweep my gaze across the room. Little white folded things have invaded every surface, including the floor. I lift my foot away from nearly crushing one. "What is all this?"

She picks up the one on the table she'd been working on then slowly retreats to the bed. Her expression says she's not sure if she should trust me, or something. The air is thick with all the apologies I should be making. And she doesn't even know the half of it.

"I'm making a thousand paper cranes." She clears space on the bed by moving the creatures, then folds her legs under to sit. Her hands work the paper.

"Okay." I'm not sure if this is concerning or not.

She sighs. "I think I have two hundred and twenty."

I set her chair back upright. She *sounds* okay. But whatever's going on in this room is not normal. "But you need a thousand."

"Yes." She finishes folding then motions for me to bring her another of the square pieces of paper from the table.

I bring it to the bed then hesitate, peering down at her on the snow-white comforter. I am 100% sure that getting into bed with Grace is the wrong thing to do. But she's looking up at me with bleary eyes as she slowly reaches out to take the paper from my hand.

Those soft brown eyes are searching my face.

I climb onto the bed, up on my knees, avoiding the paper cranes and still looking down at her. I want to take the paper from her hand and gently lay her back and then start worshipping her body the way I told her I would. The way I keep thinking about. Instead, I settle into sitting, facing her and mirroring her crossed legs.

She breaks our locked stare to focus on her folding. "The crane is called the *bird of happiness.* Its wings supposedly carry souls to heaven. It's believed that if you fold one thousand cranes—it's called *senbazuru*—your wish will come true." She looks up. "I started when Mari died. It's stupid, of course—"

"No, it's not." I want to kick myself for not being here sooner.

Her gaze travels to all the birds around the room. "No, you're right. It's not. *Senbazuru* isn't a silly thing. It means something." Her eyes find me again. "A Japanese girl who was a victim of the bombing at Hiroshima—one of the *hibakusha* named Sadako Sasaki—started folding a thousand cranes. Her wish was to live, but she died before she could finish. Others completed the work."

The tangle of emotions in my chest is making it hard to breathe. "Your wish is to have your sister back."

She smiles. "No. My wish is to have my *family* back." She sighs and cradles the half-finished crane in her palm. "Folding a thousand cranes is a symbol of hope. And healing. The statue of Sadako at Hiroshima Peace Park holds a paper crane in her hands. My mother brought Mari and me to see it when I was the same age as when Sadako died— twelve." She looks to me again. "I thought I could heal my family by just being... *better*, you know?" Tears glisten at the corners of her eyes, and I'm dying inside. Dying to hold her, but I'm frozen in my spot, watching a tear leak out and run down her cheek. She's not wiping it away, and I don't feel like I should either. "As if I could just be successful enough, if I worked hard enough, I could fill the hole that Mari left. But I can't. My father works through his grief in the office. My mother…" She presses her lips together and shakes her head. "She's closing down the exhibit, Theo."

I can't help it—I have to touch her. I gently take her hand that's not holding the crane. "The exhibit she and your sister built?"

She nods. "My mom wants to lock Mari away in the past, but…" She gestures to the origami all over the room, tears chasing each other down her cheeks. "She's still here. Still a part of us. And I haven't finished my thousand cranes yet."

I'm choking up, but I squeeze her hand. "Teach me."

She chirps a laugh, holds the crane in her fingertips, and wipes her face with the back of her hand. "You want to learn origami?"

"I want to help you fold a thousand cranes." And I do—desperately. This suddenly feels like something I can do, a legitimate way I can help Grace heal. What's going on with me—with my crazy need to be free—can take a back seat for a while. What's important is getting Grace through this. That's the only way I'll be free, anyway. I can't leave her maniacally folding origami cranes all by herself. It's just not right.

Grace is searching my face again. "You're something different, Theo."

I smirk. "You don't know the half of it." But my whole body is lighter now that it feels like we have something to do. I climb off the bed, retrieve a bunch more folding papers, and bring them back. Grace has finished her crane, so she starts teaching me. My first two attempts look more like spastic butterflies. She doesn't make fun of my sad craft, just slowly, patiently, shows me where I'm going wrong. She's constantly folding her own as she teaches me. Eventually, I get one that looks halfway right. She gushes with enthusiasm, which is over-the-top and too much… and it makes me grin. And want to make the next one perfect.

We fold for a while in peaceable but intense quiet.

And then something magical happens. We've shifted to sitting side-by-side on the floor, and the motions are now automatic. And soothing. Almost meditative as one fold follows another, a crane emerging from a flat piece of paper over the course of a few minutes, then starting another. We make lines of them along the top of the bed, then marching single file in a silent parade around us. I start putting them on Grace's legs, to see if she can fold while keeping them perched, birds on a wire. She wordlessly takes up this challenge, and only when I've folded enough that there's no more room does she start lining them up on *me*. I'm hopelessly bad at it—can't even keep one balanced on my thigh through a single folding.

Grace plucks it from the floor where it tumbled, again, and puts it safely up on the bed. Then she stretches, arms reaching overhead, interlaced fingers massaging each other. I do the same, wondering how long we can keep going. Grace reaches for another slip of paper, and I do as well. I'm in this for as long as she is.

"Theo?" We haven't spoken in so long, the sound sends a pulse of shock through me.

"Yeah?"

"What would you wish for?" She's focused on her folding.

I sneak a look at her. "These are *your* cranes. I'm just helping."

I can't tell if the furrowing of her brow is concentration or displeasure with my answer. She finishes her crane and twists to put it on the bed. I feel the heat of her stare, so I stop folding and look up.

"What did you want to talk about?" she asks.

I give her a quizzical look. "We can talk about anything you like."

Her intense look doesn't waver. "You said in your text there was something you wanted to tell me."

Shit. "Oh. Um…" I focus on folding again. "It's nothing."

She puts her hand on mine, the one folding, and stops me. Then she takes my crane, sets it aside half-finished, and holds my hand in the two of hers. Her touch is electric enough—we haven't bridged the space between us nearly the whole time I've been here—but then she starts *massaging* my hand.

I keep my groan inside. "Okay, *that* feels really good." My hand cramping dissipates under her touch, but my skin is heating up.

She smirks. "You *will* talk. You are powerless to resist my sexy ways."

She has no idea.

"You don't want to hear my complaints. It's just family stuff." The heat is spreading, flaming my cheeks and reaching down. I have to look away from the way she's working my flesh with her hands, or my cock's response to this will be impossible to ignore.

She releases my one hand only to reach for the other. That one's even more cramped, and I legit have to stifle a moan. She's intent on her work, massaging the meat of my palm, then pulling on each individual finger. I focus on breathing normally.

"If you don't start talking…" She gives me a dead-sexy stare that goes straight between my legs. "…I might have to move on to other body parts."

Fuck me. "Okay, okay." I swallow but don't move to pull my hand away. "I have a big, well, extended family. They're very focused on, um…" It's difficult to concentrate with her lacing her fingers between mine and drawing them through. She seems to sense that—or maybe she's noticing the tightness in my pants, which I'm powerless to stop—so she halts the intense massaging and just holds my hands in hers.

"They're focused on what?" she says softly, eyes on my face now.

"Marriage," I say because *mating* isn't the kind of thing you say outside the lair. Not until potential mates are brought into the world of magic. Grace has already been there, but I still don't know how much she remembers… or wants to. "Kids. They're really focused on the kids."

"They're pressuring you to settle down?"

"It's more than that." I don't know how to explain any of it—mating, soul mates, the magic that will happen if we make love—without forcing her to confront what's happened. "It's like my only purpose is to breed the next generation. Which is really not fair—I mean, they mean well. They want me to be happy. But there's this pressure to do it now. Right now. Right away. And with the person who's been… preselected for me." Even that sounds worse than it is. "The *right* person."

She frowns. "Who's the right person?"

You are. Of course, I can't say that. "The one that's been chosen."

Her expression is fierce as she squeezes my hands. *"That* is fucked up."

I huff a laugh. It's so strange to talk to her about it, even this way. "Yeah. But my dad's especially determined."

"Is he like super traditional or something?" Her eyes are on fire with righteous indignation but also an intense curiosity.

"Not exactly." I fumble for a way to tell it that's

true even if it's not accurate. "A long time ago, he rejected the woman who was chosen for him— really just kind of put it on hold for a while—and then she died in a fire when he wasn't there. It was pretty horrible. He went for a long time all alone. I think it was like self-punishment, you know? Eventually, he met my mom."

"Ah! But that was love, right?" She's very into this story.

"Sure." I wince. "My mom and dad *do* love each other. A lot. But she was chosen for him just like the first time." Because she's the same dragon spirit, only reborn. And her soul would keep being reborn, over and over, throughout time, until they mated. Or until the dragon died, wasted away because he never fused with his other half.

The soul mate thing is definitely weird.

She shakes her head. "Okay, but you can't live your parents' lives. Or make up for your dad's past mistakes. That's not fair or right or even, I don't know… *healthy*. What happens if you just say no? Tell them it's the 21st Century now. You have your own life. They can't force you into an arranged marriage."

"No, they can't." This weird mix of heartache and soaring fills my chest. "But I'd be disowned.

Have to go my own way. Which is fine. Great, actually. I'm 100% good with making my way in the world. That's what I *want*. To choose the life I want to have. I just… I'd have to leave behind everything I know. All of it. And they're…"

The anger drops off her face, and her eyes go wide. "They're your family."

"Yeah." But it's a relief to say it out loud—and to her. Even if she doesn't know all the facts, at some level, I know she understands. Or maybe she *will* once I figure out how to leave.

"Oh, Theo." She releases my hands and reaches to hug me. "That's so fucked up."

"Right?" She's hugging me hard, but it's awkward, sitting here surrounded by paper cranes.

She leans back. *"Fuck.* Between my mom and the exhibit and your family and this arranged marriage bullshit… it is time for an ice cream break. Come on." She springs up to her feet and offers me her hands.

I take them and climb to standing. "Can't argue with that." My heart is lighter than it's been through this whole thing. Not that I've told her anything, but it *feels* like a confession.

In the kitchen, Grace has an impressive collection of ice cream pints in the oversized freezer.

"*Coffee Crisp. Green Tea Pistachio. Rum Raisin. Charred Banana.* What's your pick?"

"Those are ice cream flavors, right?" Teasing her is suddenly a lot less dangerous now that I've confessed my dilemma.

She squints at me like she's reassessing my mental competence. "Don't diss the Morgenstern's. If you're a vanilla guy, just say so."

"I'm definitely a vanilla guy."

"Hm." She starts pulling out pints and having me hold them. I max out at eight, but thankfully, she finds what she's looking for, buried in the back. "You're in luck. *French Vanilla.* Probably not totally freezer burned."

"Yum." The pints are freezing spots on my skin, but this is one of the few moments of pure happiness I've had recently. A couple times yesterday, snuggled under the blankets. Today, while folding cranes. And now, juggling ice cream pints. My smile dims a little as I realize what all those have in common.

Grace scowls at the French Vanilla. "On second thought…" She tosses that into the nearby sink and burrows back into the racks of the freezer. She says something, but it's muffled because her head is literally *inside* the frosty upright. Her quest, whatever it is, gives me a moment to admire her backside, which is perfectly displayed by the yoga pants she's been wearing this whole time, but which I didn't appreciate quite as much as I should have until now. But then, I didn't have this view before.

"Okay!" She pops back out, and I scramble not to be caught staring. *"Black Pepper Molasses Vanilla!"*

"Is that good?"

She squeezes her eyes shut in orgasmic pleasure and mouths, *So good,* as she holds the tub with both hands. This does terrible things to my bliss state. My mind is instantly putting Grace back in bed, making that face as she squirms under me. She moves on as if it were nothing, setting the vanilla down, adding the pistachio to it, then storing the rest, one by one, back in the freezer. She grabs two spoons out of a drawer, hands one to me, and only then notices the look on my face that I'm clearly failing at hiding.

"What?"

"Nothing."

"Are you always this strange?" She grabs the two tubs and hands me the vanilla.

"Probably."

She shrugs and beckons me to a small table at the end of the kitchen. It has a spectacular view of the city out a tall, thin slit of a window. We've been folding so long, the sun is low in the sky, bringing a hazy warmth to the view. We settle on the chairs and tuck into the ice cream.

"So, what do you want to do?" Grace says around an enormous bite. "You know, if you tell your family to fuck off and you get to choose the life you want to have."

"Write my stories," is my automatic response. But that's not right because I would write them regardless. "I mean, I guess try to publish? Maybe? Hard to support myself on that, though. I don't know—maybe PA work. If I can get it."

She turns her spoon upside down to lick the ice cream off, then she points it at me. "I still want to read them."

"You really don't." I'm equally terrified and thrilled at the prospect. Which is crazy.

She narrows her eyes. "Don't tell me what I want." Then she digs another heaping spoonful out of the tub and shrugs. "Unless they're horror or some twisted torture porn. I'm not into that."

Torture porn? "They're about dragons." It feels dangerous to tell her this.

She looks up from her contemplation of the ice cream. "Oh! Like your name. *Wyvern.*"

"Yeah." Definitely dangerous.

"Is this an *autobiographical* dragon story?" She waggles her eyebrows. "And is there sex? Because then I *definitely* want to read it."

I swallow. Because there is, and I'd somehow forgotten that, momentarily. I take a breath and let it out slow. Am I really going to say this? "They're about humans who can shift and become dragons. They're an endangered species just trying to survive. The stories aren't about fighting monsters or slaying evil... they're about finding yourself in the middle of a destiny you didn't choose and deciding what kind of dragon you really are."

She sets down her spoon, staring at me. "So... what kind are you?"

My heart stops... and then restarts when I realize she doesn't mean it that way. *Not literally.* "The kind that wants to do the right thing. And tell stories. But those two, sometimes, are in conflict. It doesn't seem like I can do both." I keep looking at her lips, trying not to, and remembering how they tasted.

She nods like this is very serious. "And these dragon people—they have arranged marriages." It's not really a question.

"Yes." My heart is still thudding around, not doing me any favors.

She carefully puts the lid back on her pint of ice cream and folds her hands under her chin. "Your stories are part of you, Theo. No matter what, you have to write them. And *share them* with the world."

I half-smile, in a nervous way. "I don't know about that."

"You can start with me." She rises up and collects up both our pints. I've barely touched mine, but then the only thing I'm truly hungry for is sashaying across the kitchen to put the ice cream back in the freezer. She returns to the table and offers both of her hands, pulling me out of my seat. She gazes up at me. "I know what it's like to put yourself out there with your art. I know how hard it is. Let me be the first to see them. I promise I'll be gentle." The double entendre is there, but soft. Like she really means it.

"Okay," I hear myself saying before my brain comes up with all the reasons I should say no.

She smirks and turns to lead me from the kitchen, still holding my hand. We're heading back to the room with the cranes, which is good. We've got hundreds more to fold—

Grace stops suddenly before we reach the door. She turns back, pulling me close with our clasped hands, peering up at me. "You don't have to do this. Folding endless cranes."

"I want to."

She shakes her head, eyes glassing up like she's going to cry. "I know what kind of dragon you are, Theo." Her voice is soft. Her hands are suddenly on my chest, making my breath catch. She slides them up and behind my neck, drawing me down into a hug. I bend down, unable to resist this call of her body to mine. Her cheek presses to mine, and she whispers in my ear. "The kind who saves people." Then she kisses my cheek as she draws back, only she doesn't go far, stopping just short of pulling away. "I was right the first time." Her voice is a whisper, her face just inches from mine.

Everything in me says to kiss her. "About what?" The way she's looking at me, gaze bouncing between my lips and my eyes, says *Kiss me hard.* But if I start... I don't know if I can stop.

She smiles a little and finds my eyes. "About being best friends." Then her fingers weave into my hair, and the look she gives me isn't just an invitation—it's an opening of her heart. I can feel it, resonating through the connection we already have. The connection I've been fighting since that moment the witch paired us. I should let her go. I should release her right now and walk away, right out the door.

Instead, I pin her up against the wall with my kiss.

Her gasp is like gasoline on the fire roaring to life inside me. Her mouth opens, and I claim it, my tongue tangling with hers, dominating as my hands skim her body, hungry for all the touch we've not had. Her hands grab onto my shoulders, urging me closer. I press my entire body against hers, her back up against the wall, my hand reaching down to help her leg hook over my hip, opening her so my cock —*so fucking ready*—grinds through our clothes to just the right spot. My hand fists her hair, breaking the kiss, and opening her neck to me. I bite down, not too hard, just enough to tell her I'm fucking serious about this.

"Oh, God! *Yes.*" But her gasps are lost in my urgent need to touch her. I feast on her neck, eliciting more cries as my hand slides up her thigh, wishing to magic that our clothes would simply disappear. I would plunge my cock straight into her, right here, up against the wall, and... *Holy fuck, what am I doing?* The thought crashes through the haze of blinding lust. I can't do this! I can't even come close. She doesn't know anything. She's unprepared, vulnerable, still healing. *Fucking stop, Theo!* I'm not devouring her anymore, but I can't seem to wrench my body away from pinning her to the wall. I'm aching for her so badly...

Grace grabs at me, trying to urge me into the very thing I can't do. Her hands slide down my body, and her fingers dig into my rear, urging me to grind against her like I was a moment before.

"Grace, I can't," I pant, pulling away from her neck, but she still has her hands deep in the rear pockets of my jeans. "I just can't—" I pull back completely, disengaging from her and the wall and all of it... and realize too late what's happened.

Grace has pulled the train ticket from my pocket.

SEVEN

Grace

"YOU'RE LEAVING?" MY BRAIN IS SHORTING OUT. *Theo just kissed me*—no, he gave me ten seconds of hot loving up against a wall like I've never had— and he's got a train ticket to LA. In his pocket. Leaving today.

"I can change the ticket." His hands are in his hair like he wants to pull it out. Instead, he throws his hands out wide. "It's not what it looks like."

I slowly hand the ticket back to him. "But you're leaving." I reach behind me for the wall—it's still there. Solid. Unlike the ground shifting under my feet.

It was too good to be true. Too good to last. The first glimmer of happiness I've had—real joy, not the fake kind where I forget for a few minutes that

Mari's dead—and it was going to abruptly end. Without warning. Just like everything else.

"Grace, I am *not* leaving you," Theo insists, but I can barely hear him over the rushing in my ears.

My brain puts the pieces together even though I don't want it to—I don't want to know. "You're going to be with *her.* The one your family chose."

"*No!*"

It's so sharp, it yanks me out of my haze.

"*Grace.*" He takes hold of my shoulders, and I almost shove him away, but I don't, I just stare up at him. "*You* are my soul mate."

"What?" I look at him like he's crazy because *what the fuck?*

He releases me and presses his hands together, holding them to his lips and stepping back. "You don't remember. Do you?"

A wave of dizziness sweeps over me, but I've got the wall to brace me. "Remember what?"

He starts gesturing like somehow that will make me understand. "You were out when we rescued you. When *I* rescued you, Grace."

What is he talking about? The set?

"We brought you back to the hospice center at the lair—"

"Wait, what?" *Lair?* What the fuck is he—

"—but you were in a bad way. The doctors wanted to keep you for a while, said it was better if I didn't visit, but then you *woke up*, Grace."

"*The fuck* are you talking about?" A panicky feeling is banging around in my chest.

"I'm trying to tell you." He looks like he's about to cry, which makes no fucking sense. "You woke up, and somehow, you and Jayda found each other in the hospice. And she demanded the doctors let you go. And of course, we couldn't keep you—*wouldn't* keep you—we're the dragons who *rescued* you..." But he's trailing off now, looking more upset, and I realize he's reacting to me—to my face. Because it's frozen in horror.

Because I remember.

I remember the hospital.

I remember the torture.

I remember the aliens and their crystal mind-fuck probe and the screams. All the screams.

"No." I shake my head and jab a finger at him. "*No!* You were *not* there."

"No, I wasn't." He looks ashamed about this. "I should have been. But they thought—Niko, the Lord of our Lair thought—it was better if you didn't see me. Not yet. Not until... I could..." He stops and looks like he's going to be sick.

I try to move away, but the wall holds me prisoner. "J-Jayda brought me back. Jayda rescued me."

"No, Grace." His shoulders drop. "The dragons did."

My head is shaking *no, no, no.*

"I'm a dragon. You are my soul mate. You're the one destiny says I should be with." He just sounds defeated now. "The Vardigah—the monsters who captured you—they tortured you *because* you were my soul mate. They tried to destroy you, but you were too strong, Grace. You're *dragon spirited—*"

"Get out!" It erupts from me like a vomit of words.

"Please let me explain."

"Get out, get out, get out!" I yell it while my fists fly at him, pounding on the massive steel of his chest—the chest I thought was a safe harbor, the steel I thought would protect me, but all of it was just lies and lies and more lies. "Get. The. Fuck. Out!" I'm shoving him now, toward the door of the apartment. I can barely see him through the tears, but the blurry mess that is Theo shrinks under my blows. As if I could hurt him. As if there's anything I could do to move him if he didn't want to go. Instead, I glare at him, tears streaming down my face, fists clenched at my side, like the sheer force of my will can make him leave and take all his lies with him.

He stumbles back, collides with the wall, then turns the corner, heading out.

I stand there, trembling, barely able to breathe through the gasping, hiccoughing sobs, until I hear the front door open... and then close. I wait a moment more, terrified he might change his mind and come back. But he doesn't. Then I stumble down the hall to Mari's room, bracing my hand on the wall. My whole body is numb even as it quakes. I blink away the blurriness, although the tears keep leaking out. Hundreds of paper cranes cover the room, like the madness slipped out and turned into birds. I cross the floor, careful not to step on them with my bare feet, then carefully, one by one, I move them aside, making room on the bed. When there's enough space, I curl up, hands fisted under my chin, lying on my side with my knees tucked up.

I let the sobs shake me.

The birds shake too, white, quivering paper on the snow-white spread.

Eventually, I run out of tears. They dry on my face, and I force my stiff hands to uncurl so I can brush at the itchy salt left behind. My breathing slows, my mind still empty. Unthinking. Not feeling. I'm like a blank canvas in the wake of a terror-storm that wiped me clean. Slowly, one thought at a time, my brain comes back online.

The torture was real. *It happened.* I know this, but ever since Jayda brought the three of us home—her, Daisy, and me—I've just stuffed it away like it was a crazy nightmare. Jayda went right back to work, so I did, too. Mostly. Okay, I *tried.* What I avoided like it was molten lava was trying to make sense of it. There was no explaining what happened to us any more than you could find a reason why a meteor hit your house and not the one next door. It just *was.* And it was crazy, so I could tell no one, which spared me from having to explain it, least of all to my parents, who were still in mourning. They easily bought my lie about skipping out of town on a lark. Because that's who Grace is, right? Frivolous and irresponsible. Besides, life was back to being *real* again, so everything would be fine, right?

But nothing is fine.

And Theo… this hot boy who comes along and kisses me and insists the nightmare was *real*… and that it's back, and here's a story about it, and I just *can't.* It's crazy. All of it. I want it to all just *go away.* I want life to be *normal* again. But it's not. I freaked out about a fake patient getting fake-shocked on a fake-hospital set. I've screamed at Theo and sent him away for daring to insist any of it was real. I'm obsessively making cranes like folding paper will fix everything.

That's not normal, Grace. I know this.

I draw in a shuddering breath. And another. One, two. In, out.

Slowly, tenderly, I probe the time after the torture. Toward the end—and I didn't know it was the end at the time; I was sure I would die there—I was passing out a lot. The creatures… what did Theo call them? Vardigah. It sounds like some stupid thing from a fantasy novel, but whatever. The *Vardigah* were ramping up. There was no under-standing them either, except that they were pissed. And trying to break our minds. I think they halfway succeeded with me, for a while, but mostly, I just passed out. Then they'd leave, and I'd wake up, and then they'd come back again. But one time—the last time—I woke up in a hospital bed instead. A real one, not the nightmare kind. My filthy clothes and my one red sneaker were sitting in a bag on the floor—someone had changed me into a soft hospital gown. And the door wasn't locked! I remember that first, the tremulous feeling of hope. The hallway was quiet and empty when I peeked out. Then I heard Jayda's voice coming from one of the other rooms. I hustled over and saw her for the first time —eyes sunken, her brown skin ashen, her natural hair limp and hanging down. She was arguing with a man in a doctor's coat. When she saw me, that's when she demanded he bring us to Daisy. Which he did, but she was in so much worse shape. I didn't realize until then that she was older even than Jayda's thirty-two. I still don't know. Maybe forty-five? She was beautiful in the way of someone whose spirit is truly free—only this spirit had been nearly crushed. The torture had taken her down hard. Jayda demanded to know where we were, and when the doctor refused to say, she insisted that Daisy be moved to Mount Sinai.

They agreed. Only something happened...

I pull in a breath and sit up. *We never left that hospital.* I press my fingers to my temples, trying to remember, but no—we didn't leave. Or, more precisely, I don't *remember* leaving. We were waiting for an ambulance or something to come transport Daisy, and somehow, I must have fallen asleep, but the next thing I remember, we were there—*Mount Sinai.* All three of us, checked in, and waking up in side-by-side beds in the ER. Jayda and I were released after a bunch of tests that showed nothing but dehydration, but Daisy never woke up. She's still there, as far as I know. A wave of guilt propels me off the bed and to my feet. I know Jayda's keeping tabs on Daisy, but why haven't I visited? Why didn't I check on her myself? What kind of World's Worst Friend am I??

But I know the answer—I didn't because I couldn't.

I wasn't strong enough.

Something about that stirs around inside me, and I teeter for a moment, light-headed. But as that passes, I spy a glimpse of red in Mari's closet. I must have not closed it the whole way when I was rummaging through for more folding papers. I step over the cranes and slide open the mirrored closet door. On the floor are my red Converse shoes.

When the alienss—no, the Vardigah—kidnapped me, they snatched me right out of my bedroom. I put up a fight. That was how the shoe came off. When I returned, it was still in my room, lying tipped over on its side. I put it with the other one, here in the closet. I could slide the door closed and pretend they didn't exist. With these safely locked away, I could telescope my life down to only the safe things—things that wouldn't make me cry or hurt or *feel*…

Or I could choose to live again.

I reach down, pull the shoes from the closet, and slide them on.

The ride to Mount Sinai isn't far—just a few stops on the uptown train, and I'm there. I'm lucky it's visiting hours, and they let me in, even though I'm not family or anything. A shudder runs through me at the antiseptic scents and gleaming metal of the hospital machines, but I'm okay. I can do this. When I get to Daisy's bedside, she's sleeping… and a man is sitting in a chair by her side.

"Oh," I say because I'm so completely surprised, I can't think of anything else.

He smiles wide as he rises. He's incredibly beautiful, like the leading man in a show about youthful Greek tycoons, and he moves like *swagger* is just part of his DNA. The tiny lines at the corners of his slate-blue eyes somehow make him look sexier. I have no idea who he is—does Daisy have a husband? I suppose he could be a brother.

He gives me a soft look as he passes. "She'll be glad you visited, Grace," he whispers.

I gawk at him as he glides through the door and out into the hall. *He knows me.* I look back to Daisy, but she's out. She couldn't have told him anything. A chill runs through me. He's one of them—one of Theo's dragon people. And he's here. *The dragons rescued you,* Theo said.

Shit. The disorientation is crowding my mind again, squeezing on my chest. I'm not pushing that away, but at the moment, I need to check on Daisy. I shake it off and shuffle into the room. She's deeply asleep—the same "sleep" as when Jayda and I found her in the other hospital. *The one run by dragon people.* What did Theo call it? A hospice. Which I don't understand, but I'm not dismissing anything as *unreal* anymore. The damage the Vardigah did to Daisy was real. The circles are gone from her eyes, probably because of whatever is in the IV attached to her arm, but she's still out. Still running away to the interior of her mind.

Or maybe trapped there.

I slip my hand in hers and squeeze. "I'm sorry." Tears sting my eyes again. It's a wonder they let me into the hospital—I have to look like a wreck. "I should have come sooner."

She doesn't stir. Her honey-blond hair lies limp on the pillow. The delicate pale skin of her cheeks seems a little less death-like than the first time I saw her. I don't even know the color of her eyes because

I've never seen them open. But I remember the kindness of her voice. Jayda was our rock—she was strong when the storm of the torment was battering us. But Daisy was our *hope*. She was the one who insisted that all would turn out well in the end because the Universe had a purpose for us, and we hadn't fulfilled it yet. She was all about mystical things and nonsense and that freaking Tarot she kept doing imaginary readings with… and she kept the light going in that horrible, dark place.

I kneel down and press my forehead to her hand. My tears are dripping on her now, and I'm going to be super embarrassed if a nurse comes in or the hot dragon guy returns, but they don't. The Universe gives Daisy and me a moment. Then I wipe away the tears and straighten.

"We made it out," I say to her softly. "Now you need to come back to us, okay? It's time, Daisy." She doesn't move or make a sound, but somehow, I just know she hears me. I squeeze her hand again. "I'll be back tomorrow. You just hold tight."

Me and my red sneakers walk out of the hospital and into the fading sun of the day.

There's somewhere else I've been avoiding… and that I need to visit.

EIGHT

Theo

OH GOD, I'VE FUCKED UP SO BAD.

That thought keeps banging through my head on an endless loop, crowding out any others. I'm so distracted, I can't find the station entrance. It's like I've lost my mind.

I stop, close my eyes, and just breathe. Standing on a street corner in Chelsea doing absolutely nothing doesn't seem to disturb anyone. No one bothers me.

Think, Theo. *Think.* I pull out my phone and text Grace. *I'm so sorry. Please text back. I need to talk to you.* I don't know why I bother—she hasn't answered the last three I've sent. She's pissed. And upset. And really, really freaked. She was full-body trembling when I fled, panicked and aghast at what

I'd done. I was supposed to *help* Grace… and all I've done is make things worse. *I'm such an idiot.* And I've screwed up even more by running away. I should have stayed at her apartment until I could make sure she was okay. I tried to go back, but the door had locked automatically behind me.

And she won't answer my texts. *Fuck.*

I could go back to my apartment. Maybe Ree would have some clue what to do. I discard that idea as soon as I think of it. I could call Niko, but teleporting into the apartment? That's a straight-up horrible idea. Bringing up dragons is what shut her down. Me, resurrecting all the things that hurt her, all the torture she endured because she was my soul mate… I can't show up like the Vardigah did. But she's totally cut me off. I don't know if there's anything I *can* do.

Fuck. Me.

This is gutting me in a way I didn't think possible. People stream around me, rushing on with their lives, avoiding the obstacle that is me standing stock-still on the street corner, going nowhere. I have a weird sense of being out of my body, like my soul is struggling to leave it and rush back to Grace up in her sky-high apartment, where she's crying, in pain, hurting in a way I'm helpless to stop. I suddenly understand what my father must have felt when he discovered his soul mate had died in the fire that consumed the Athens lair. They weren't mated, so he didn't die with her, but he wasn't there to protect her. Her pain was *because of him,* even if he didn't set the blaze. It must have torn him apart. There are some things you only get one chance at, and while that wasn't strictly true for mating—my mother died and was reborn, they literally got their second chance—it's still true for *people.* Each individual life. You only get one chance to do the right thing by them. And if you fail, you have to live with that.

I can't live with this.

I look at the phone in my hand. Maybe I should call 9-1-1, just to get someone in there...

Jayda. I literally smack my head with my phone. Grace would let Jayda in, no matter what. I quickly send her a text, *Have a minute? Need to talk.*

In a meeting, comes back right away.

It's Grace. She's upset. Kicked me out. I run my hand through my hair. Where is Jayda's office? I vaguely remember she's working in an auxiliary office in Midtown, not down in the financial sector. Now that my brain is working again, I easily spot the closest station entrance and hurry that way.

Then you stay the fuck away from Grace. Jayda's text is like a gut punch.

No, no, no. *I'm worried. Just text her. Make sure she's okay.*

I take the stairs two at a time and swipe my MetroCard through the turnstile to end up on the platform just as the train's pulling in. It's an express toward Uptown, so I hustle aboard with everyone else. My route app would help if I knew where I was actually going, but I just make a mental note to get off at 50th Street.

As the train lurches into motion, Jayda's text comes back. *WTF did you do? She's not answering my text.*

I wrap my arm around the pole so I can type. *I can explain. Riding the train to Midtown. Where can we meet?*

It takes her a long stretch to reply, but then she sends me the address of a coffee shop. I plug that into my app. I'm on the right line, thank God. A fraction of the tension in my chest eases. Grace trusts Jayda. Jayda cares for Grace. She can fix this unholy mess I've made. Please let that be true.

Once I'm off the train, I have to hoof it to the Bird and Branch Coffee Shop, which is several blocks from the line. When I get there, Jayda isn't in the outdoor seating area, so I hustle inside, where everything is bright white, from the painted-brick and peg-board walls to the mosaic-tiled tables to the bright overhead lamps nestled in greenery. I find her standing by a small round table next to the front window, her crisp black suit and white blouse almost tailor-made for the décor. The place is small but full, with limited seating and most people in line for their caffeine hit. Jayda has a cup in hand, but she's holding it away from her body, either to keep it off the suit or possibly to throw it at me.

"Sit your ass down and tell me what you've done." She says it quietly between her teeth, so we're not attracting too much attention.

I grab a stool and sit as instructed. Jayda sets her cup down as she expertly navigates the tippy wooden stool hands-free and in heels. I've never understood how women can wear shoes like that without breaking their ankles, but Jayda acts like her professional attire is a second skin, fully inte-grated into every move. It's that hidden power and sense of physical ease I sensed before, but that's not intimidating—it's the condemnation in her eyes that hits me hard.

I swallow and try to keep my voice low. "I told Grace I was her soul mate."

Jayda jerks back, eyes wide, and it's a good thing she set her cup down, or it would be all over her suit. Then her eyes narrow, and she sweeps that assessing gaze over me, the one taking in everything from my jeans to my t-shirt and coming up with... "You're one of *them?*"

I sigh. I know she knows—about dragons and soul mates and all of it. Niko himself tried to talk her out of bringing the three of them—her, Daisy, and Grace—back to the city. She was having none of it. Niko said she didn't believe him. And it wasn't his place to reveal his dragon to her. That was her mate's job.

"You insisted on leaving the hospice," I say, trying not to put too much accusation into that. "We couldn't keep you. *Wouldn't* keep you. But you can't expect me to not worry about my soul mate." I have to be careful here—I don't want to blow whatever cover Akkan and Ree have. Although, I doubt either has had to construct a story yet. Ree hasn't even made contact.

"So, you stalked her back to the city?" It's like she can't believe what I'm telling her. "What is *wrong* with you people?" She gestures at me like she doesn't know what to do with me. "Grown men, acting out some make-believe story about dragons and elves and magic. Why should I trust anything you say? For all I know, you're one of the 'elves' out of costume!" She makes mocking finger-quotes.

At my shocked look of protest, she quickly leans across the table and jabs a finger at me, almost knocking over her coffee. "You *shut it.* I don't want to hear any of your bullshit about dragons and soul mates and whatever else there is in this insane cosplay game of yours. You hurt my friends—"

"I didn't—"

"And how am I supposed to know that?" She clenches her fist and presses it to the table. I think she wants to shove it in my face. "How do I know you're not here to take us back to that place…" And then she runs out of steam, shuddering and wordless, like they're suddenly jammed up in her head.

I cringe inside. Because if Grace is hurting, of course, Jayda is too. She just steamrolls right over that, so it's easy to forget. But it's there. The memory of it. The pain. And I just jammed a red-hot poker into the middle of it.

I put my hands up, placating, and I soften my voice. "Jayda, I promise you're safe." Ree should be saying this to her, but he's not fucking here, and she needs someone to say it.

"Of course, I'm safe." But uncertainty flickers in her eyes. "I'm in the middle of Manhattan in a coffee shop." But she knows better than that. I don't know how or where the Vardigah came for her, but it was somewhere in the middle of Manhattan. Probably when she was alone in her apartment, like the others.

"I promise you—they can't find you anymore. We... *the people like me* captured the witch—the *woman* who was their wayfinder." I flick a look to the line. There's one younger woman who's pretending not to eavesdrop on us, but the rest seem oblivious. "They can only track places, not people," I say to Jayda, dropping my voice further. "And they don't actually know where your apartment is—the witch, er, woman led them directly to *you*. Without her, they'd have to search the entire city to find you again, and they obviously can't do that, given what they are." That's the best explanation I can come up with in a coffee shop. "But I knew Grace was struggling with the aftermath of all of it. That's why I came down here. To watch over her. And it's a good thing I did." I give her a pointed look. "She couldn't handle the set. It reminded her too much of... you know. And now I've screwed up and told her the rest too soon. Because I'm an idiot and just… mixed up. I don't know what I'm doing, and she wasn't ready. Now she's freaking out, and I'm scared. She's not answering her texts. She's locked her door. I need your help. Because I can't be the one responsible for hurting her. I just… *please.*"

Jayda's retreated a little, leaning back, folding her arms… but the fear is gone from her eyes. And the condemnation is too. "You care for her."

"Yes." I throw my hands out then scrub them through my hair. "Yes, I care for her. She's my soul mate. I know that doesn't mean anything to you—I know you think I'm just some, I don't know, nutjob with a twisted hobby—but it means something to *me.* I don't know if she's okay—in fact, I'm sure she's very *not* okay—and it's killing me. Please, Jayda, will you help?"

She sighs and shakes her head. "I can't believe you told her those goddamn stories."

"I'd hoped *you'd* already told her. At least, some of it."

"Me? I'm trying to *protect* her from your crazy, not invite it into the house!" But she's less angry now and more… I'm not sure. Mollified somehow. "But now that you've gone and done it, I'm not leaving Grace twisting in the wind." She pulls her phone from the pocket of her suit and checks it. "All right. I was giving her until I met with you to text me back, but seeing as how that's not happening, we need to escalate this."

Massive relief flushes through my body. "Should we call 9-1-1? I'm afraid that will just freak her out like the ambulance."

"No!" She gives me a look like she's reassessing my intelligence. Again. "I have the code to her door, remember?" She arches an eyebrow. "I'm assuming she didn't give it to you?"

I shake my head. Because obviously.

"Mm, hm." She rises up, and I quickly follow. She drops her full coffee cup in the trash and leads the way outside. She's striding in those killer heels— I guess she didn't have time to change into sneakers this time—and I keep pace, but I'm feeling bad that I'm making her walk all over Midtown.

"Should we call an Uber?" I ask.

"Train's faster this time of day." And she's right —the sun is going down and the streets are filling up. She keeps striding toward the station, head held high and determined. I already know she's Ree's soul mate, but the way she's so protective of Grace —it's easy to see the *dragon spirit* inside her. It's true of Grace, too. She's fighting to survive, fighting to heal. The thousand cranes are just the kind of thing a dragon spirit would do—struggle on, daring to hope. I'm carrying a stabbing pain deep in my chest because I've made that harder by throwing too much at her—knowledge she wasn't ready for—and it's all because I'm an inexperienced dragon who doesn't know what he's doing. *Fuck me.*

We board the train and ride it back downtown to Chelsea. Jayda doesn't speak, just keeps tensely checking her phone and occasionally texting, but it must be work because when I give her a questioning look, she just shakes her head.

When we reach Grace's apartment building, Jayda stops me before the elevator. "Maybe it's better if you stay down here." My wordless torment for that—I can't think of any good reason I should go up, but I'm dying inside—moves her. "Okay, *fine.* But let me do the talking."

I nod my fervent agreement as we step in. "Tell her whatever you need to. Tell her I'm an asshole or a lunatic or whatever. I'll follow your lead. I just want her to be okay again." The elevator lurches into motion.

She gives me a pinched look. "You're really in love with her. Or feeling tremendous guilt. Which is it?"

I gape for a moment. "I…" But I stall out. Is

what I feel for Grace *love?* Or is it just that reflexive soul-mate protectiveness? The kind that panics when something bad happens to the literal other half of your soul.

Jayda's eyebrows lift. "Okay, then."

"It's just guilt," I rush out.

She snorts a laugh and strides out of the elevator. *"I'm* doing the talking here. You're a mess."

"Agreed." I mean, she's not wrong.

Jayda gets out her phone and taps through to the app that click-unlocks the door. She knocks as she swings it open. "Hello? Grace? It's me, Jayda." Silence is the only answer. She and I aren't exactly sneaking through the apartment, but I'm holding my breath as we hustle through the main room, check the kitchen, then head down the hall to the bedrooms. Grace is nowhere to be found. It's like she just... left. The only thing different is a space on the bed in Mari's room has been cleared of cranes, and there's an impression on the pillow where Grace's head must have been.

The tear stains hollow me out. I'm just standing and staring, paralyzed, when Jayda walks in. "What in God's name is going on here?"

It takes me a second to realize she means the paper birds. Which objectively looks like a crazy person went wild with origami. "We were working on it together. Folding a thousand cranes."

"Why?" She's picking her way across the floor in her heels, heading to the table.

"Hope." I look back to the pillow and feel it emptying my soul. *Where have you gone, Grace?*

"Well, this explains why she's not texting us back."

I turn to see Jayda holding up Grace's phone. "That's good… I guess?"

Jayda scowls. "You're sure those assholes in the elf costumes can't find us again?"

A spike of fear pierces me. "Pretty sure."

She's unimpressed. "That's *not* what you said at the Bird and Branch."

My shoulders hike up. "I don't know how they would find you." And I *don't* like that she left her phone behind. But before my brain can get too far into panic mode, I realize there's one thing weighing on Grace's mind even more than dragons and elves and the fact that I've been lying all along about who I am and why I'm here. "But I think I might know where Grace has gone."

NINE

Grace

I HAVEN'T BEEN HERE SINCE MARI DIED.

Murdered. Sometimes, it's hard to say the word, even in my head, because there's no resolution to it. No justice. No murderer captured and put on trial and sentenced to life in prison. Just… Mari is dead.

And her work is here, at the exhibit in our mother's gallery, gathering dust.

I stand in the doorway for a long time. As the sun's last rays fade behind me, I finally unlock my legs and go find the light switch. The spotlights in the racks above shine on the white walls, diffusing light everywhere. The pale blond wood floor reflects their glow, making everything bright. It's an extreme contrast to the framed pictures. Some are on the walls while others hang in the middle of the room, held up by nearly invisible wires to the ceiling. White pedestals support plexiglass boxes with artifacts interspersed throughout the gallery. Everything is lined up neatly. It has the effect of marching you down the center, but you can slip off to the sides, between the rows, to find secret treasures. I know why it's this way—Mari explained it between Netflix binges on the couch. The layout is similar to the internment camps. *Relocation Centers.* Each had their own unique aspects, but the relentlessly sterile rows and columns of the barracks were the same everywhere.

As was the barbed wire, which Mari strung along the top edges of the walls.

Our great-grandparents were at Heart Mountain, Wyoming, and Mari told their story through the pictures and artifacts passed down through the generations. She also sought other internees, looking for more art created during internment. Impromptu art and architecture schools were set up in some of the camps—older internees, often *Issei,* Japanese immigrants, would teach the camp's children, the *Nisei,* second-generation. Torn from their homes, forced to relocate with only what they could pack and carry, not knowing if or when they would be released, they worked with what they had to make life tolerable.

To create hope for their children.

I wind through the barracks-like rows of images. Our great-grandfather, Harushi Tanaka, was just twenty, but already an amateur photographer. He smuggled in his camera and film—they were illegal in the camps. Developing had to wait until after the war, but he captured so much of the life they lived. The barren rooms, with a single lightbulb and no furniture except cots and what they could fashion from scavenged wood. The communal cafeteria and poor-quality food. The beautiful gardens the internees themselves planted and tended, so they could have decent vegetables to feed themselves. The guard shacks and their barbed wire and machine guns, pointed in.

Michiko Ikari, my great-grandmother, was one of Harushi's favorite subjects. Pictures of her fill the exhibit—in the silk-screen shop where she earned a tiny wage, sitting in the camouflage-net-covered classroom for art classes, and my favorite, one where she holds a painted, carved wooden bird in her hands. The picture hangs next to a dust-covered plexiglass case with the ten birds that survived through the years. Mari had them restored, their colors as sharp as when Michiko first painted them. We still don't know how she managed the paint, much less the lacquer that originally covered and protected them.

I lift the plexiglass cube and set it on the floor, then carefully pick up a brilliantly red bird. It's the same one in the photo, and as I cradle it in my hands, like Michiko did seventy-five years ago, holding it for the man she would later marry, I can see my reflection in the glass. I've always thought I looked like a female version of my father, with his proud Japanese features, but now I see that genetics skipped a few generations and gave me my great-grandmother's nose and her slightly-full lips and the mischievous look in her eyes. Her picture has a simple placard next to it. *"Gaman:* to endure the seemingly unbearable with dignity and patience." Michiko crafted her birds in the spirit of *gaman*— she used her talents to survive, emotionally, and even find love in this bleakest of times. Something deep inside me settles with a sense of finality, like a resolute period at the end of a sentence.

I can't let this exhibit close.

I return the bird to its spot then replace the cover, carefully brushing away the dust.

Then I turn back to the picture of my great-grandmother. "I promise," I say to her. My sister poured her heart into this. It's the story of how the Japanese Americans interned in the "Relocation Camps" had an impact on art after their release and for decades after. It's the story of art and hope and perseverance in the face of fear and bigotry. *It's the story of my family.* I don't know how, exactly, yet… but I will make sure this exhibit opens and is shared with the world, just as Mari intended.

"Grace?" The voice startles me, but I recognize it right away, even though the hanging pictures have blocked my view of the door, where it came from.

"Jayda?" *What in the world?* I step out to the center of the gallery. "Oh." That's all I manage when I see not just her but Theo, too.

"Honey, are you okay?" Jayda's casting a wary look at the pictures and barbed wire as her heels *click-click-click* down the center aisle. Theo trails behind her, holding back, practically shrinking inside himself. Which baffles me until I remember —*I threw him out.*

"I'm okay." I wait for them to reach me.

"Theo thought you might be here." Jayda scrubs her examining gaze over me. "Honey, you don't *look* fine."

I have to be a wreck, what with all the crying. I

glance down at my red sneakers then back up. "I went to see Daisy."

Her eyebrows fly up, and she and Theo share a look. "Is she still…" Jayda lets that hang.

"Yeah." I swallow and straighten. "She took the torture harder than we did. I'm worried about her."

Jayda sighs, long and deflating. "Me too." Then she pulls me into a hug that feels long overdue. I hug her back, hard. "You had us scared," she says, still hugging me. "Don't do that, okay?"

I nod into her shoulder, but tears are surging up again, and I don't want to mess up her pretty suit. I pull back and swipe them away. They're just left-overs, residuals from the emotional floodgates that opened and dumped out everything I've been holding inside, hoping I could just lock it all away and forget about it.

I sniff and say to Theo, who's still lurking at a distance, "I'm sorry I freaked out."

"No, I'm sorry," he rushes out. He steps closer, then stops. "I'm an idiot for… I shouldn't have dumped all that on you."

I shrug, but then Jayda leans forward and mock whispers, "He kinda *is* an idiot, Grace. Listen to the man when he tells you who he is." Her smirk is hidden from Theo, who looks even more stricken, and it all just makes me laugh. Not a big laugh, just one of those tiny ones that erupt when your emotional filters are down.

But it feels good.

Theo still looks uncertain, so I tell him, "It's okay. *I'm* okay. I mean, I *wasn't*... but I'm better now."

The relief on his face is so sweet. *This guy*... I'm still not sure how all the pieces fit together, but every step of the way, every small thing I've needed, he's been right there, like a guardian angel.

"Okay, then." Jayda's giving me a strange look. "I actually have a whole pile of work waiting back at the office. I'll probably be there all night." She points her finger around the gallery. "I definitely want to know what this business is all about, but if you're okay right now, Grace, I'm going to head back to Midtown."

I frown. "Sorry to interrupt your work. Again."

She pulls my phone from her suit pocket and hands it to me. "Yeah, well, answer your texts. And make sure Theo walks you home." She gives me a tight, slightly knowing smile, then another hug, and then she's *click-clicking* her way out of the gallery, leaving me alone with Theo.

He steps forward, hands out in apology. "I really

am sorry. And I still want to help you fold those cranes. Will you let me? Please?" He glances around the gallery and does a quick double-take at the picture of Michiko on the wall. Then he looks back to me. "And I can help with anything here that you need."

There's a warmth blossoming in my chest. I think it's the kind of thing you feel when someone so obviously is doing you a kindness—not out of obligation or guilt, but because they actually care. I don't know much about Theo's world, even though it crashed into mine pretty spectacularly, but I do know that *I'm* the thing he was running away from. And he has every right to—no one should have to marry someone just because their family expects it. And yet here he is, checking on me, making sure I'm okay and offering to help.

It's the kind of thing a best friend would do.

I bite my lip, not sure I'm entirely ready, but my heart's already been cracked wide open today... and that let out the fear festering inside. "There *is* something you can help me with."

He steps closer again, eager, but then stops. "Anything."

"I *will* need help with those paper cranes," I start. "And I've decided to finish the exhibit. I don't know how…" I glance back at the display with the carved birds. "But I need to make something in the spirit of *gaman*—to find a way out of the darkness—like my great-grandmother, Michiko."

Theo edges nearer and peers down the row at her portrait with the bird. "Is that her? She looks so much like you."

That makes me smile. "And I need you to teach me about dragons."

He blinks and draws back. "What?"

"You said you're one of them."

"Yes, but…" He stalls out, looking slightly panicked.

I shake my head a little because it's *crazy*. "Can you really turn into a dragon? I mean… what does that even look like?"

He's speechless for a moment, blinking several times through the surprise. "I *can…* " A bit of smile tugs at his lips. He checks out the hanging pictures around us. "I'll need a little more space, though."

"Hold up, you get *bigger?*" This is just nuts. Although I *do* remember he was unusually heavy, especially when he was pinning me to the couch with that hot kiss.

His eyes sparkle, and it's not just the lights. "Yes."

My face scrunches up. "Doesn't that violate physics or something?"

"Almost certainly." He's barely holding back the smile.

I wave my hands at him. "Well, go on."

He looks around the gallery, but the distribution of hanging prints must not fit his, well, *needs*, so he grabs my hand and tows me to the middle where the largest open space is. Then he releases me and picks up a pedestal topped with a camp-made vase enclosed in one of those plexiglass cubes. The display cube isn't that heavy, but those pedestals are weighted down to keep them steady—and he picks it up like it's a basket full of air. And gently too. The vase doesn't even rock as he moves it out, clearing space.

Then he grabs the edges of a picture hanging next to me. "Okay, if you hold this print back..." I grab hold and pull it back, just a few feet, which is all the swing of it will allow. "That's good," he says, then positions himself in the now-cleared area. It's maybe ten feet of open air on a side, but the room is taller than that—my mother sprung for a floor-and-a-half of space, insisting a proper gallery needed lots of negative space to focus the attention on the items contained within. And that space, right now, contains one hot guy taking off his shirt. Theo's watching me watch him, his gaze locked on mine as he drops his shirt to the floor.

"So, uh…" I'm rendered incoherent by the beauty of the man. I mean, I *knew* he was solid muscle under there from the first day, but to see it displayed before me… "We should bring that pedestal back, and you can just stand on it. Pretty sure that'll bring in the crowds."

He smirks. "It's easier to shift without clothes on."

My heart stutters. "Are you stripping all the way down because…" I swallow. "I'm not sure I'm prepared for that."

He chuckles. "You're prepared to see my dragon, but not to see me naked?"

"Yes. I think that's exactly right."

He dips his head and gives me a look that's sizzling hot. "They kind of go together."

"Do they?" I want to fan myself, but my hands are occupied, holding back the giant frame. It's a picture of Michiko pouring tea into camp-made ceramic cups. I can't decide if it's disrespectful that I'm thinking more about *thirst* than the solemnity of traditional tea service in the camps right now.

"Are you sure you're ready for this?" Theo's

voice draws me back, and it's softer now. He's frowning.

I tighten my stance, holding back the frame to give him room. "I'm ready."

A shy smile flashes across his face… and, in a blink, he changes.

Into a giant black dragon.

"Oh, shit." I stumble back and completely lose my grip on the picture. It swings and bangs into his solid black mountain of scales while I fall on my ass. A split second later, the dragon is gone, and Theo is rushing to my side. Naked. Completely naked. So much skin and… *holy shit, this boy is well-endowed.*

He's kneeling down to help me, a wild look of concern on his face. *"Grace!* Are you okay?" His arm is so freaking strong as it slips behind my shoulders to help me sit up. But he's *so close* with all that muscle, his chest spread before me… I just gape. And look down. *Yes.* That is definitely the finest piece of man hardware I have ever personally observed.

"Pants," I literally pant. I drag my gaze up to his. "You need pants."

He has the funniest look on his face—like he's not sure if I'm losing it or just funny—but he releases me from his prison of hotness and pivots away as he rises up. Because otherwise... *Sweet Hottest Man Alive:* The Full Monty. I watch his insanely tight ass walk back to where his pants lie in a puddle on the floor.

I feel you, pants.

After he puts them on, my brain reboots. I climb to my feet, face flushed with both the heat of Theo and the embarrassment of acting like such a drooling idiot.

But there's one thing that's certain: Theo really is a dragon.

He turns back, shirt in hand, a smile playing across his face. "What do you think?"

What do I think? "I have so many questions."

His smile broadens, and it warms me straight down to my toes.

TEN

Theo

"So, we literally share a soul?" Grace asks me.

She's perched in her spot on the couch, back at her apartment—not sitting, but literally crouched in the corner, chewing on her fingernail, like she's coiled up, ready to spring. But it's a good kind of tension. Excitement, I think.

"Not exactly." The real answer is *not yet*—not until or unless we're mated—but I don't want to go there. Leave it to Grace to drill down immediately to the hidden nuances of things. She's *sharp*—and not just that wit of hers, but the savvy behind it. "We each have one *half* of a soul. When a dragon is born, his soul is broken. He keeps half and the other half fuses with the soul of a baby girl born at the same time."

"Hold up, we share a birthday?"

I smile. This is safer territory. "April 26th, right?" It's in her file—the one Niko made for every soul mate paired to a dragon, just for accounting. And to help the dragons as they embark on their romantic quests.

"That's just freaky," she says.

"Sometimes, it's a day or two off." I shrug. "We only know what it says in the *Mýthos tou Drákou*—the ancient book of dragon lore Niko saved from the fire."

"The one that destroyed your home lair in Greece two hundred years ago."

I nod. We've covered a lot of territory since yesterday's dragon-reveal at the exhibit. I answered her questions all the way home last night, but I didn't stay—*couldn't* stay. We were both emotionally wrung out, and I didn't trust myself not to end up in Grace's bed. But I was back first thing this morning because we have *work* to do—cranes to fold and an exhibit to flesh out. She's been peppering me with questions the whole time. It's an incredible relief to have this out in the open, now that Grace seems to have embraced it, but I'm still worried that it's having some hidden, corrosive effect. Yet she seems more settled, at peace somehow, than I've ever seen her. She's still thoroughly energetic, like usual—especially about the exhibit. Which I really want to get back to.

"So, the fire almost destroyed your species, but now you're coming back." She's still going. "And *that's* why everyone's so hot for you to make the dragon babies."

Dangerous territory again. I wave my clipboard at her. "Can we get back to the script for the exhibit? I've got some questions—"

"Wait, how many dragons are there?"

"I don't know the exact number—"

"Approximately."

"Fewer than a hundred."

"Whoa." She rocks back until she slumps against the couch. "That's really small." All the bright-eyed enthusiasm has fled.

I toss my clipboard on the couch and climb up with her. When she's like this—even the tiniest frown—it's like I'm compelled to be physically near her. "Look, forget about the dragons." I brush her hair back from her face and tuck it behind her ear —just because I can hardly help touching her when I'm this close. Which is also why I keep my distance, pacing the floor while she sits and sitting whenever she gets up. Grace doesn't need me pawing at her—she needs help with her *gaman* project for the exhibit. "I love that you care—I truly do—but the dragons can take care of themselves. Especially now, with everyone paired up with their soul mates."

Her eyes go wide. "They're already making dragon babies?"

I laugh a little and shake my head. "Some of them are mated, yes. But it hasn't been that long. Most haven't even managed to meet their soul mates yet. They're still figuring all this out." *Like us,* I want to add, but I don't—because she doesn't need that pressure from me.

But her gaze is a million miles away, her brain chewing through something. "*Mated.* You mean married." Her gaze sharpens and suddenly swings to me.

"Sure. I mean, no, it's not the same. Mating is permanent. It's… complicated." The last thing I want is to go into all that. I tip my head to the side and give her my best puppy-dog eyes. "Can we work on the script now?"

She takes a deep breath and blows it out. "Sure." But she looks uncertain.

"What's wrong?" I cringe inside—I ask her that way too often. Like I'm just waiting for her to freak out or melt down or have a panic attack, and that's really not fair. I don't want her to think I'm on edge around her—the complete opposite is true. When I'm here, I'm fine. It's when I'm lying awake in my own bed back at my apartment that everything comes undone in my head.

She usually brushes it aside, but this time, she answers, carefully picking at the threads of the throw blanket that's across the back of the couch. "I'm worried the Vardigah will come back."

Oh, man. I scoot closer and squeeze her shoulder. "You're safe. I promise."

She peers into my eyes. Hers are soft brown, rimmed in black, and sometimes, when she looks at me like this, vulnerable and open, I feel my soul trying to reach her across the gap between us. It's almost a physical pull, and it's all I can do to keep my hands off her.

"When I was there," she says, "I didn't think it would ever end. I didn't think it was real. And when it was over, it was just easier to pretend it wasn't real, you know?"

"I know." That need to move closer is surging.

"Now that I *know* it's real, I can't help thinking they'll come back."

The urge is too strong—I cup her cheek with my hand and move close enough I can bring her into my arms if she needs that. Or if I can't stop myself. "They *can't* hurt you."

"I know you said they can't track people without the witch—"

"They can't hurt you because I won't let them." I vow it with my eyes, with my touch on her cheek, and I'd swear a blood oath if I thought it would convince her.

Her eyes go a little wider. "You'd turn dragon and fight them."

There's a trembling need in me for her to understand this. "I would *destroy* them."

She closes her eyes briefly and shudders. I can't tell if that's good or not. Then she opens her eyes, and there's something new there—something yearning and hot enough that I draw back. Either that or I'm throwing her down on the couch and making love to her right now.

"Because I'm half your soul." It's a whisper, but I feel it all over my body.

"Yes." That part's been true from the beginning

—before I ever said a word to Grace, back when I just watched her from afar as she put her life back together. Had the Vardigah come for her, they would've had to go through me. But now? Knowing the trauma they put her through, how it *hurt* her when she was already struggling? I'd tear the Vardigah limb from fucking limb. My rage would be off the leash. That's something more than just a reflex. I don't want to name it because I'm afraid of what that means.

I clear my throat. "Do you want to fold more cranes or…" I pick up the clipboard with my notes. "Should we get back to the script?"

She drops that intense gaze and nods. "We should work on the script."

I climb off the couch again because I'm *way* too close to her. "Okay, we're set with the opening scene. I got a message back from wardrobe on the *Scrubs of Chicago* set—they know someone who can pull together a period costume for us really quick. And you look just like your great-grandmother. With the spotlight starting on that picture of Michiko, then fading to a spotlight on you, a simple bio intro will hook the audience right from the start." It was Grace's idea to do a skit, bringing her art in to complete the exhibit and draw in an audi-

ence for opening night, but she needed a writer…
and, well, that's me.

She stands up from the couch, and in an instant,
she's slipped into character—chin slightly lifted, her
hands cupped in front of her, holding an imaginary
bird. "My name is Michiko Ikari, and this is my
story."

"Exactly." I draw the pencil from the board's
clip. "You were a senior in high school, your family
was forced to relocate, and now you're in the camp,
making the best of things. That gets us oriented." I
look up. "Okay, I need something that launches you
into a separate world—a world within a world. You
said you worked in the silkscreen shop?" I'm
keeping it all in-character because Grace said it
helps her to remember the stories her sister told her
while she was doing her research for the exhibit.

"I took the job for the money," she says, face
grim. "It wasn't much, but it helped buy seeds for
the garden and paints for Harushi."

I point my pencil at her. "The boy you're interested in. So, he painted as well as took
photographs… mainly of you. That's a great way to
bring him in and start their love story." I scribble
some notes. "Tell me about the work at the shop," I
say as I write.

"We were printing flyers and posters for the U.S. military—the same people who forced us from our homes and kept us behind barbed wire with machine guns pointed at us, day in and day out."

I look up. "You're kidding me."

She doesn't break character. "It was a job. I did what I had to."

I nod and jot down more notes. "Did you meet Harushi at the shop?"

"No, but we also printed menus and flyers for events at the camp—Harushi was one of the artists who helped design those. He refused to work for *them,* but he would help *me* if I needed something for a project."

I look up from my clipboard and smile. "And he took pictures of you."

She gives me a very solemn look and lays a hand on my arm. "We had to be discreet. He was older than me—*twenty-two.* My parents would not approve. Both our love and the camera were illegal."

I pretend to be scandalized, but this is perfect. "But you *were* in love with him."

She nods, once. "Very much. Which was why it was so hard to see him go off to the war."

"Wait, what?" Now I'm genuinely horrified. "You didn't mention that."

She releases me, and righteous anger fills her entire body, hands clenched, slender shoulders quivering. "They drafted the internees right out of the camp. We were so horribly suspect—we *looked* like the enemy, after all—that we had to be torn from our homes, lose everything, and be shipped in a train like cattle from California to Wyoming. But when they needed more soldiers for the war, apparently, our blood was red enough to spill."

"What the hell?" But this obviously *has* to go into the story. "They *drafted* Harushi?"

"There were others before him—protestors who refused to be drafted while their family's civil rights had been suspended. But then the guards took them away, tried them, and sent them to prison. I told Harushi that prison was *safer* than the front. But when his draft number came up, he kissed me and promised me he would live. And that he would marry me once the war was over."

I'm just shaking my head and writing as fast as I can. "Unbelievable. How could they…" I just let that hang, cursing under my breath while I scribble on. Then I stop and look up. "He lived, though, right? You're the proof of their love."

She looks shocked for a moment, breaking character. Then her eyes glass up. "Yes. I'm the proof."

I'm afraid I've screwed up again. I pull her into my arms and hold her, awkward with the clipboard in my hand. She burrows her face into my shoulder, and I can feel her pulling in breaths, the quiet sounds of not-quite-crying.

After a long stretch of seconds, she pulls back. "It's okay. I just…" She looks up at me with tear-brimmed eyes. "I want to read your story, Theo."

"You're going to *act out* this story." I miss her in my arms already. I'm so fucked with that.

"No, the other one—about the dragons." She sniffs back the tears, but she's serious.

And I couldn't say no to her if I wanted to. "I'll… send it to you."

"Now," she says like she thinks I'll weasel out of it.

I give her a small smile. "Tonight. Right now, I need to write Michiko's story."

She sighs but gives me an accepting nod.

So I write and write, and Grace acts out every scene as I do. We fine-tune it, take a break for paper crane folding, then get back to it. When we're too tired, we huddle under the blanket and watch Sabrina. But when Grace falls asleep on my shoulder, I gently ease her onto the couch and sneak out. I tell myself, on the way out, that spending the night with Grace is nothing but trouble—a distraction she doesn't need, and a heartache I can't handle right now.

It's a lie, but a functional one.

Back at my apartment, Ree's got a bed partner —I can hear them from my room, even with the door closed—and I'm dying to know if it's Jayda. I can't decide if I want that to be true or not. I pull out my phone and text Jayda my status update. *Still have to finish the cranes, but we're ready for the show.* Grace has already activated her mom's network of supporters of the arts, not to mention the media, about the sudden grand opening of the exhibit scheduled for the day after tomorrow. Jayda knows about all of it. Two more days... before I have to face what all of this is leading to, for better or worse.

A text comes back from Jayda. *How's our Gracie doing?*

I smile at the *"our"* then cringe because whoever's in Ree's bed, it's definitely not Jayda.

She's good, I text. *I left her sleeping on the couch.* Then I realize how that might be taken, so I add. *No chill, just Netflix.*

Her emoji reply is definitely laughing at me. *That's your business. Just remember: I'll murder you if you hurt her.*

I smile. *Understood.*

I'm exhausted from the day, and tomorrow will be a long one. Then the show is the evening after that. But Ree and his bedmate are going to keep me up a while, and I made a promise to Grace…

In the bottom of a drawer in a chest full of them sit five weathered, purple notebooks. I haul them out and set them next to the computer. I told Grace I'd send it to her, but it's a mess. And handwritten. And an embarrassment of unfinished character arcs and sloppy side quests and meandering philosophical tracts that aren't fit for the light of day. I kept telling myself I'd edit it into something decent someday. Revisions make the story, right?

I sigh. Then I remember Grace facing the pain of the past—of her family, her people, and herself—and her admonishment. *How can you be a writer if you don't let people read your stuff?*

I think, *Theo, don't be a coward.* Then I boot up my laptop, open Word, prop open one purple notebook with another… and type.

There once was a dragon whose fate was sealed the moment he was born.

ELEVEN

Grace

"ARE THE CRANES SET?" I'M TUCKING IN THE 40's-era blouse that Theo miraculously procured for me.

"I just checked them." He helps me slide on the cardigan sweater that goes over the blouse. I've already changed into the rest—a red flower-print skirt, white ankle socks, and my red Converse sneakers. The shoes are the only non-period part of the costume, and they stand out. They're my personal touchstone, where I connect with my great-grandmother's past and march it forward to the present. At least, that's the idea.

"You sure the shoes are okay?" I ask. We're in the warehouse at the back of the gallery, off stage, so to speak. My mom's managing the performance area, a roped-off section in the middle of the hanging photographs—the same spot Theo shifted into a dragon and changed everything.

"You look amazing." He's gazing down at me with that tender expression that's starting to do strange things. Like make my stomach flutter. Or flush me with warmth all over. It's not lust. It's not sexy at all. It's a kind of *pride* and *approval,* and it flusters me *badly.* I've never had anyone look at me the way Theo does. And my heart can hardly deal with it.

I pull in a centering breath and let it out slow. "Okay. Time to do this."

"One more thing," Theo says, pulling me from my mental prep for slipping into Michiko's character.

"What's that?"

"Don't freak out."

I scowl at him. "What did you do?" We've been practicing endlessly over the last three days. I've got my lines down solid. I've been living in Michiko's head for the last twenty-four hours, fine-tuning the script and doing a dress rehearsal last night. But it's showtime—this is not the time for last-minute changes.

"I invited some friends." He's biting his lip, looking nervous.

I glance at the still-closed door to the gallery, then lean closer to him. *"Dragons?"* I say it in a whisper.

He huffs a laugh then smiles. "No." Then he gets serious. "People from *Chicago Scrubs.* Cast and crew."

"What?" My heart lurches. The door looks a lot more menacing than a moment ago.

"They've been asking about you," he explains. "Worried about you. I kept telling them you'd be back to the set eventually, but I didn't want you to feel rushed. And you shouldn't—feel rushed, I mean. They wrapped up the pilot, and they have to see if the series is greenlit before they're doing any more shooting. So, you don't have to worry."

"I'm not worried about that." How can I worry about a career I've flamed out of? Going back to the set never even seemed like an option. "It's just… embarrassing." I sigh and shake out the nerves by clenching my hands and then flicking them open. "These people have *not* seen me at my best."

"Which is why it's great they're here tonight." His voice is soft, and it draws me out of my jitters, calming me. He's always had that effect. And I realize that he's done this on purpose—he's invited them to give me a chance to show that I'm better.

"You're doing it again." I reach up and softly pat his cheek.

His eyes go wide, almost panicky at my touch. "Doing what?"

"Being my personal Prozac." I drop my hand from his face even though I want to give him an enormous hug and melt into that broad chest of his.

His shoulders relax. "You're going to do great. I'll be right up front. Your personal tech crew."

Then I can't help it. I wrap my arms around his neck and hug him hard. It's not like we haven't shared a few hugs over the last couple days. And lots of cuddles. No hot kisses, though, so I know that's off-limits. Theo's seeing me through the opening of the exhibit because he wants me to work through my pain. He wants me healed from the Vardigah's torture and working through grieving for my sister. I know it's all temporary—he's got bigger plans in LA or somewhere, doing something that's definitely not pinning me to a wall with his molten-sex kisses. He's a good friend—the best of friends— but I know that's all he wants, no matter what the "fates" have decided for him. He didn't choose to be my soul mate. And I would never want to trap him into anything. That's just fucked up.

This is the lecture I've been giving my heart for

the last three days, sternly warning it not to fall in love with Mr. Hotness. Not that my heart ever listens to my head.

"Thank you," I whisper to him then pull back. "For all of this."

His killer smile comes out and shines down on me. "Wouldn't be anywhere else."

For now. My heart fills in that part because, apparently, my heart is also a jerk and a masochist.

"I'll see you after the show." Theo smiles, squeezes my hand, and leaves me to get in character while he scurries up to run the spotlight and the rest of the props.

I pull in another calming breath. Then I picture what it must have been like, over seventy-five years ago, when my great-grandmother was told that she had to leave her house and her friends, taking just what she could carry in suitcases, and move with her parents to Wyoming. All because the country was at war with people who looked like her. How she faced an uncertain future—one already filled with heartbreak and that promised even more—and she lifted her chin and worked hard and, most important, *kept going.*

I peer down at my red shoes. *Hold tight.* Jayda and Daisy and I would say it over and over. It was our mantra. Our sanity. But when the storm has passed, you have to let go in order to move forward.

I push open the door to the gallery, and with measured, solemn steps, I find my mark in the middle of the roped-off area. The crowd is intense. Every space is filled. My mom brought in a carpenter crew to rig the hanging photographs so they could be raised for the performance then lowered later for the exhibit. The gallery is now one large open space, and the only portrait that hangs in the middle is the one with my great-grandmother holding her carved, wooden bird. Theo's spotlight is trained on her until I find my mark and stand, chin lifted, staring into the crowd with unseeing eyes. They're a shadowy force, hidden by the glare of the lights. They're my friends—Jayda's here in addition to the cast and crew from the show—and family—both my mom and dad—and a bevy of media and celebrities, the kind that only my mom and her star-power could assemble. They're here to witness the past, but they will see more than that—because my heart is in this, and that'll soon be obvious.

The spotlight on Michiko fades out, and mine fades in.

"My name is Michiko Ikari, and this is my story." I recite my lines, baring my heart with each one. I draw on the pain inside, the thing that sits in the bottom of my stomach and in the back recesses of my mind, painting it on my face for the audience to see. To mirror. Because that's what humans do—when we *see*, we *feel*. For so long, I've felt apart from my own family, my own history—Mari and Mom and Dad were the architects and artists who carried the legacy of our family forward into the future. My connection was tenuous at best, mostly through my sister-love. But now I forge my own connection. I craft it with my own kind of art—the art of *drama*, of being seen and evoking emotion in others. I show the story of Michiko's love for Harushi. How she smiled for his camera. How she carved a bird just for him. And how she cried when he left for a war that had imprisoned them both and for which he would risk his life just to win his freedom.

There is no audience behind the glare. There is only this story, and the words and movement and emotion I pour into it to bring it to life. At the part of the story that tells of the release from the camps, I bring out the carved red bird tucked in the pocket of my skirt. I hold it in my palms just like in the photo Harushi took of Michiko seventy-five years ago.

"A thousand wishes are carved into this small

creature." I pet the bird with a single finger. "A wish that Harushi will return from the war. A wish for us to marry and have a family. A wish for Harushi to find a school that will accept Japanese-American students so he can become the architect he wishes to be. It's just a small thing, but it was made in the spirit of *gaman*. We have borne the seemingly unbearable with dignity and patience. And those thousand wishes, once released, came true." I lift the red bird in my hands. The spotlight widens to show the thousand white paper cranes we've made, each suspended in air by a slender, invisible string and attached to a motorized track on the ceiling. As I spread my upraised hands wide, the cranes take flight. The crowd gasps as the thousand wishes spread out over their heads, fluttering with the motion and the currents of air, as if actually in flight. I drop my arms, quickly tucking the carved bird away, and shifting my voice into narrator mode. "The influence of interned Japanese-Americans, once released, on the world of art, architecture and design has been immense. Despite discrimination in housing and jobs, internees went to school, worked hard, raised families, and used their skills to beautify the world. Japanese-Americans designed the Twin Towers and the Corvette.

People who spent their teens and twenties in the ten Relocation Centers emerged to bring to the design world *shibui*, which means 'craftsmanship, intelligence of design, understanding of materials, and imagination.' Harushi and Michiko built their lives and their family in the aftermath of the war. They endured the injustice, they bore the unbearable, and they, like so many others, went on to have a great influence on America, right to the present day, including the exhibit in which we are standing. We invite you to remember the past…" The lights rise as the photographs descend from the ceiling as if summoned from history. "And never forget. So we might never again imprison our own people based on fear alone." The words are Theo's, but the heart of it is mine. And I see that heart reflected in the faces of the crowd, now illuminated, as they clap and clap, some with tears in their eyes.

I keep my composure, solemn-faced, but my heart is soaring. I may not be a great actress—I'm certainly not a famous one—but *I can do this*. This is real. And the smile on my mother's face, across the crowd, as she's congratulated by her high-society friends, is all the audience I need. The applause fades, but the noise is just as loud as a hundred conversations spring up. My father leaves my mother's side and works his way to me. When he reaches me, I just hug him because I can tell he has no words for this. The hug lasts and lasts. At the front of the gallery, Theo's at the control station, reorienting the lights and shutting down the rest. Our thousand cranes will remain as part of the exhibit.

My father finally pulls back from the hug, but then he holds my cheeks in both hands. "Grace, this was…" He's still struggling for words.

"Exceptional," Theo says, coming up behind him.

"*Yes!* That's the word." My dad gives Theo a curious glance.

"Dad, this is Theo," I say quickly. "He helped with the performance."

My dad turns to him and firmly shakes Theo's hand. "Thank you, son. You have no idea how much this means to my family."

Theo seems startled by the handshake—and the words—but he quickly recovers. "It was my pleasure." He sneaks a sideways glance at me, which my dad, thankfully, misses entirely. Mostly because my mom is sweeping into our orbit with the gravity of her celebrity, trailing a host of glamorous people and photographers in her wake. I'd almost forgotten the media was here to cover the event.

I give Theo a wide-eyed *Behave yourself* glare, but he just grins.

"Grace! Darling, you were brilliant." My mom hugs me, and I know it's half performance for the audience she carries with her, but it still fills me with light. The hug is over fast, and she's smiling for the cameras, turning me to tuck me under her arm. Then she pulls my father over by their clasped hands, which could be performative, too, but I see the way their eyes meet and the shine in them, and suddenly, I'm working full time on not crying in front of the mini paparazzi my mother has assembled. After a frenzy of picture-snapping, my mother announces, "We're celebrating the 75th anniversary of the release of the internees, but this exhibit will be semi-permanent or perhaps a traveling showcase with other such exhibits around the country." Then she starts fielding questions from her friends and the local reporters. This is the part she excels in… but not me.

I catch Theo's eye—he's standing back from all the attention—and wordlessly ask for help. I barely have to plead with my eyes, and he's already by my side with a ready excuse.

"I'm sorry, I need to return Grace's costume to

wardrobe right away," he says to my mother. "Please excuse us for a moment."

My mom looks bewildered until I say, "Mom, this is Theo." Her expression morphs to understanding—she's never met him, but I totally kept her in the loop about his help in this mad scramble to pull the show together. Then someone else demands her attention, and she turns away.

Theo's hand locks with mine, and he drags me out of the figurative spotlight. The gallery is legit crammed with people, but his large frame and determined beeline for the door in back clears a path. We pass Jayda on the way, and I stop just long enough to hug her. "That was fantastic," she says, but then Theo's sweeping me away again.

We make it to the back, push through the door, and the noise of the gallery mutes when Theo closes it behind us. "Oh my God, Grace, you were amazing—"

I cut him off with a hug so filled with joy that I'm jumping up and down on him. Which is embarrassing, and the wooden bird in my pocket is poking us both, but I don't care. "Thank you, thank you, thank you."

"It was all you." He's hugging me back and laughing at my exuberance.

I have to release him, I know that, but my heart tells me to steal a kiss, so I do—just on the cheek. It's innocent. Mostly. "I couldn't have done this without you," I say because it's true. And I'm staring into his eyes, wishing he'd kiss me, but the way he's looking at me is soft and tender, not like he wants to rip my clothes off. *Settle down, Heart. That's not happening.*

"Are we going to change you out of your costume and head back in?" He raises an eyebrow. "Or do you want to sneak out? Because there's totally a back way out of the gallery."

My face heats because my mind jumps to my apartment, and Theo *helping* me out of my costume, which is wrong on so many levels. But there's no way I can be normal back in the gallery. I need to burn off this nervous, excited energy and decompress. Yet, guilt worms through me for running out on everything.

I pull Michiko's bird out of my pocket and hold it up as evidence against the idea of simply leaving. "What about this?"

Theo smiles softly. "I think you should keep it."

It never occurred to me, but it feels right. At least for now. "Okay, definitely sneaking out, then."

He grins, grabs the bag with my gear, and laces his fingers with mine.

As we head for the back door, I blurt out, "Oh! I read your novel last night when I was totally not sleeping, but *what the fuck*, Theo?"

"Huh?" His hand freezes on the back doorknob.

"Where's the *rest* of it? I need to know what happens to Drynor! What the heck kind of cliffhanger is that?" I peck at him with the bird in mock-angry taps on the shoulder.

He breaks out into a grin and pushes open the door. "I sent you everything I have edited. I'm working on the rest."

"God, you are such a tease."

He smirks, and his gaze drops, a quick brush over my body—ankle socks, floral skirt, and all—but I feel it. And it's definitely *hot*. My heart does a little dance of joy, even though he quickly looks away, down the alley we're winding through behind the shopfronts. It's stinky and kind of gross, and there's barely enough light from the one streetlamp at the end to keep from tripping over some broken crates in the middle, but it feels glorious. My mind's racing ahead to the apartment. Will we just burrow under blankets again? Can I just straight-up kiss Theo and see what happens? I'm so wrapped up in my tumble of thoughts, that I almost miss it when two figures appear in the alleyway...

Out of thin air. Literally not there, and then there. Right in front of us.

And they're... *Oh, God.*

Theo drops my hand and lurches forward. Before I can blink, he's turned dragon, the midnight black of his body blocking most of the alley. I stumble back, but I know what I saw.

Vardigah. Their long, ugly faces and pointed ears. A sight I could never forget.

Theo leaps into the air, wings unfurling and smacking the sides of the alley. A glint of talons catches the light. I'm frozen in place, unable to move or scream or run. It's dark, but I see him land, talons-first, on one of them—his scream is cut short as Theo cuts off his head.

My stomach convulses as the head rolls away.

Where's the other one? Theo's dragon swings its head, searching like I am, still frozen in place. *Maybe he ran away—*

The Vardigah appears right in front of me. I scream and blindly strike out. The bird in my hand becomes an inadvertent weapon, its sharp beak tearing into the Vardigah's face. I strike again, with intention, even harder. He growls and stumbles back, clawing at the wound.

It's just enough time for a flash of black, glistening scales and razor-sharp talons to swoop down the alley. The Vardigah slumps to the ground, cut literally in half.

"Oh, God." I cover my mouth with my hand. The bird in my other hand is covered in greenish blood, but *fuck the Vardigah…* they can't have this, too. I clutch it tighter and stagger back.

Theo's dragon disappears, and he's suddenly standing naked in front of me. The transformation is so fast, my brain can hardly register it.

He rushes to me. "Are you okay? Tell me you're okay, Grace!" He's yelling because I'm not answering, trying not to throw up all over him.

I swallow down the sick feeling and nod vigorously. "I'm okay."

Relief floods his face, but it's quickly chased away by anger. *"Fuck!"* He lurches away, and I can't figure out why. I retreat from the growing pool of greenish blood forming around the fallen Vardigah. Theo hurries back, still naked, but now with his clothes in hand. He fishes out his phone and rapidly taps at it. Who in the world can he be texting in the middle of all this?

Then he holds the phone up to his ear. "Niko! Thank God. I need you here, right fucking now! The Vardigah are here."

I hear something loud on the other end of the line, then a split second later, another man appears in the alleyway with us. I just stare at him. He's gorgeous like Theo with that same sexy European look. *Dragons can teleport?* I thought only the Vardigah could—

"Holy shit," the man, who must be Niko, breathes as he takes in the carnage. He whips his head to me, then back to Theo. "How did they find her?"

"I don't know, but we have to leave. *NOW.*"

"Right. Back to the lair?" Niko clasps his hand on Theo's shoulder, and the two of them walk the few steps to stand next to me. I just stare at them. Theo reaches for my hand, which I automatically give. The bloody bird is still clenched in the other one.

"No," Theo says tightly. "Her apartment."

Niko nods, but then my brain blanks out because suddenly we're no longer in the alleyway but standing in my living room.

"Holy shit!" I drop Theo's hand and nearly go down, it's so disorienting. He's there in less than a

heartbeat, keeping me on my feet.

To Niko, he says, "Jayda's back there. You need to get her out. And any other soul mate. Wherever they are. Everyone has to *move*. Until we know how this happened."

Niko nods his agreement. "You're not staying *here*, are you?"

"Just grabbing some things. Then we'll get out. And Niko... we need to clean up that mess in the alley. Grace's family is in that building. They don't know anything."

"Copy that." Then Niko just... disappears.

For one brief moment, my life was somewhat normal. And then the crazy just rushed back in. But I'm stronger this time. *I am.* I tell myself this as I stare blankly at the red bird drenched in green blood in my hand.

Then I look up at Theo, who has released me and is desperately pulling on his clothes. "What do we do now?"

"We get you out of those clothes, we grab whatever you can stuff in a suitcase, and we get the hell out of here." He gives up buttoning his shirt and just zips his pants.

A chill runs through my heart. My great-grandmother calls across time. *You can do this, Grace.* I look down and see it's not just the bird that's bloody— my sweater is smeared with greenish muck too. *Vardigah blood.*

You can do this. I march toward my bedroom, ready to make the best of whatever this is. I have Theo by my side. *My bodyguard.* My best friend. My soul mate.

And he just killed two Vardigah in front of me.

Whatever he says, that's what I'm going to do.

TWELVE

Theo

My heart doesn't stop hammering until we're out on the street again, on the move.

Even then, everything inside me is made of panic. My chest is tight, my stomach is solid rock, and I have this twitchy urge to shift into dragon form with every backfire of a New York taxi or the too-loud laughter of a nighttime crew out clubbing. Grace is way more composed, which is amazing and outstanding. She faced down a Vardigah, for fuck's sake! Stabbed him right in the face. I want to kiss her breathless for that, and for being so strong through all of this, but I'm radically focused on getting her to safety, and there's no room for anything else. To be honest, had this brought back her panic attacks, we'd already be back at the lair. I halfway think I should call Niko and do that anyway. I cannot figure out how the Vardigah found her. But she's never been to my apartment, there's no connection between her and that place, and as far as I know, the Vardigah still have to have knowledge of a *place* to find a *person*. Which doesn't explain at all how they found us in an alley outside the exhibit, but I can do nothing about that… except not let Grace out of my sight until we figure this out.

She's keeping pace with my manic strides down the street. On the train ride to my apartment, she texts her parents, telling them she's gone home for the night. That will buy us time until we sort everything.

We're barely two steps inside my apartment when Ree comes flying out of his bedroom. His face is part terror, part deadly wrath, and I know exactly how he feels.

"You going after Jayda?" I ask.

He doesn't even slow down. "What the fuck do you think?" He's out the door before I can say anything else, which is fine—I'm sure Niko's got someone guarding Jayda until Ree can get there. After that… well, it's hideaways for everyone until we know it's safe.

Grace is standing in my modest living room, clutching her purple suitcase, lips pursed. "Who was that?" she asks quietly. "And why is he going after Jayda?"

I hurry to her, then take a deep breath as I take her suitcase. I need to calm the fuck down. "She's dragon spirited, remember?" I say gently.

"Oh. Right." Then her eyebrows lift. "Wait, was that…"

"Ree. He's her soul mate. And he's going to make sure she's okay. You can count on it." I take her hand and urge her toward my room, so we can put away her stuff. I'll have to stay in the room with her—my heart can't handle anything else—but we can figure that out later. Neither of us is sleeping for a while, not with the adrenaline still pumping like mad. I set her suitcase in the small closet and close the sliding, mirrored door. "Sorry the room isn't much. Not like your place." I give her a weak smile.

She just shakes her head. But she's checking it out. The queen-sized bed takes up most of the room. The one chest of drawers sits opposite with barely enough room to walk between. Against the far wall is my desk with the computer still on, and my purple notebooks sprawled on top of each other.

"Is this your novel?" She's already scooting past me to check it out.

"Hang on." I catch her hand and pull her back. "That's not ready for an audience yet." It feels so good just to touch her.

She seems to feel the same because she comes back and slides her arms around my waist, pressing her cheek to my chest. "Theo."

I wrap my arms around her and wish that was enough to protect her. "I know. But we're safe here. As safe as we can be for the moment." I gently kiss the top of her head. "I'm not leaving your side, Grace. I hope you know that. I'm not letting them hurt you."

She nods against my chest, and it helps bleed the tension from my body. Then she peers up at me. "I'm sorry."

A smile tugs at my lips. "Sorry for what? You've been spectacular through all of this."

"Sorry this is getting in the way of your plans."

I frown. "Plans?"

She disentangles from our hug, not answering my question, just sitting back on the bed and nudging off her shoes. They're plain white tennis shoes to match her simple t-shirt and light cotton shorts. We left her red shoes and the stained costume at her apartment. With her feet bare, she climbs across the bed and curls up against the headboard, one pillow for a cushion.

She studies her hands for a moment, lacing the fingers and wringing them slightly. Finally, she looks up again. "I know I'm not what you want, Theo."

"What? Grace—"

She cuts me off by holding up a hand. "Just let me finish."

I scowl and work off my shoes so I can join her on the bed. I climb up, grab the other pillow, then sit cross-legged just to the side of her. "Go on." I try to keep my voice gentle, but I feel the panic surging back.

She smooths out the comforter between us. "I know this messes up everything for you." She meets my gaze again. "You were helping me get steady again. Because you're an incredibly sweet person, Theo. I know I'm your soul mate and all that, but you didn't have to do all this." She waves at the closet with her suitcase, but I think she means the skit for the exhibit.

"No, I didn't." Where is she going with this?

She drops her gaze again. "I know you were planning on heading out after everything was finished, and now you're stuck with me again. At least for a little while. You know…" She looks up. "Because the lizard people are trying to kill me."

I smile, even though it hurts. "They're elves."

"Right." She looks away again. "Anyway, maybe you can get your ticket to LA changed again…"

Oh. I'm almost relieved that's what she thinks. "You mean this?" I reach in my back pocket where I've been carrying the ticket ever since she found it the first time. She watches as I pull it out and show her. It's ripped in two.

She blinks and frowns. "I thought you were—"

"I'm not." I duck my head to catch her gaze. "Tore it up two days ago. Grace… everything I want is here."

Her expression opens, and her mouth works, but nothing comes out.

"Don't be so surprised." But I'm smiling, and everything in me is calming. I knew as soon as we started working on the script. I knew when we spent days together and never once tired of each other's company. I knew when I was dying at the thought she might not be okay. "I mean… I don't let just anyone read my stuff."

"But…" She sputters a little, and it's so damn cute. "The whole soul mate thing. You said it's crazy. Like the worst arranged marriage in the world because the Universe has picked some rando girl for you, and you're supposed to just…" She waves her hands around. "Hook up and make babies? It's nuts."

"It is." And it hurts because I told her all my fears, and now that's probably ruined everything for me. "And I couldn't see how that could possibly be anything but a horrible trap. I couldn't imagine how I could ever be free to just be me."

"And you *should* be. You deserve that." She's getting upset, and I'm afraid I've blown this.

I crumple up the torn tickets in my hand and throw them on the floor. "It's not about what I deserve." I take her hand, which is balled up on her knee, and I coax it open, lacing our fingers together. "Because I hardly deserve someone as amazing as you, Grace."

She just blinks again, surprised.

I rush out the rest. "I came here because you're my soul mate. I couldn't stay away when you were *hurting*. That's not how this works. And I'd give my life right now to protect you from the Vardigah for the same reason. But that's not why I folded a thousand cranes. Or why I helped you stage your great-grandmother's story. Or why I spent all that time cuddling with you under a blanket and wishing that maybe, if things went just right, we might have another kiss where you absolutely stole my heart, Grace. *Twice.*"

"I thought you didn't…" She's breathing hard. And I so want to close the gap between us, but I know it's too soon. "I thought you were leaving," she breathes.

"I'm not going anywhere," I vow. And it's true. Even if she doesn't feel the same. I trust no one on the planet to guard her the way I can from the Vardigah, so that's non-negotiable. And she's been wounded and needed a *friend*—so that's what I was. No way am I going to assume it'll lead to more because that's a complete dick move. This has nothing to do with being soul mates and everything to do with the amazing person Grace is—which doesn't mean she feels the same. Now… or ever. And that has to be okay. I mean, my heart's going to break, but that's my own fault. I'm not going to pressure her in any way. And besides, it wouldn't work. Mating only happens if Grace *truly* loves me. Anything else simply isn't an option.

She still looks stunned.

"I know you're not ready." I sigh. "I mean, you don't even know what most of this means—"

"I'm ready!" She practically leaps to her knees

on the bed, slips a hand behind my head, and *kisses me.*

I'm totally caught off guard, but it doesn't take long for Grace's lips on mine to kick my body into gear. I lift up to my knees as well, bring her body against mine, a hand behind her head to angle and deepen the kiss because *fuck,* I've been dreaming about this for days. Her tongue battles with mine, and I don't know who's most into this kiss, but it's getting hot fast. She makes that soft whimper sound I've built entire fantasies around, and it makes me ache. My hand on her back loosens her t-shirt enough that I find bare skin. I splay my hand across the heat of it and pivot her down to the bed, covering her body with mine as I sink even deeper into the kiss. I'm careful to keep my weight off her this time, but I'm so damn hard, she has to feel that. Then she bucks up into me, hooking her leg over my hips and grinding against me.

Holy fuck. "Grace," I gasp, easing off the kiss and the full-body sex-with-clothes we have going.

"Don't stop," she cries, her fingers digging into my shoulders to bring me back.

I can't resist. My mouth finds hers again, my hand busy skimming her thigh, her hip, trailing up under her shirt. She's clawing at mine, trying to pull it from my body. I lift up enough to allow me to slide her shirt over her bra, which is this delicate lacy thing I want to rip off with my teeth.

"Oh, *fuck*, Grace," I pant, my gaze trapped by the luscious round of her breast and the pointed peak of her nipple hard under the lace. "I want to dive into you and never come up for air."

"*Theo.*" She's frustrated, trying to pull off my shirt, but I know we have to cool this off, and fast. I can't take the risk—not with her. Dragons always have to be careful, but with a soul mate? There can't be anything "accidental" about this.

I ease off her, rolling to the side, but still trailing my fingers along her exposed belly. Her skin is so soft, I can't resist. I come back for a kiss just above her belly button and follow it with a half dozen more.

"Oh, God, *Theo.*" She digs her fingers into my hair, and I realize I'm promising something I can't deliver, not yet.

A breath shudders out of me as I pull away. "Grace, the things I want to do to you…"

Her eyes are dark fire. "Yes! Please! Are you going to make me beg? Because I will totally do that, if that's your thing."

A laugh bubbles inside me. I bite my lip as I

scoot up to face her, side by side on the bed—well, she's mostly on her back, hands gripping the bedspread with frustration while I try to not touch her and aggravate her anymore.

"I'm not trying to tease you," I apologize. "But Grace, my love, there's nothing *casual* about sex with a dragon."

She jerks up onto her elbows, glaring at me. "I am fucking *serious* about fucking you. Right now."

Oh, my, God, I love this woman. "Grace—"

"And what makes you think this is *casual?*" She's rocketing up to *pissed,* and I really don't want that. "I've been lusting after you since I first saw that hot body of yours, but this isn't just that. Is it?" I see the tremble in her lips, and it hits me in the gut.

"No." I bring my hand to her cheek and brush her lips with my thumb, just to stop the quiver. "It's not just lust. Not for me." I peer into her eyes. "I want to kiss you senseless and make you scream my name, but it's *dangerous* to fuck a dragon, and I won't put you in any more danger, period. I'm so far gone for you, Grace. I can't have you hurt because of me."

She blinks and sobers a little, the frantic need in her eyes settling. I don't think for a second it's just lust for her, either, even if she's not in love with me

—we're both emotionally raw, and she's had an open heart-wound for the entire time I've known her. It's part of why I'm so careful with her. Gentle. Helping the wound to heal so she'll be able to love someone again, able to open herself up, even if it's not to me.

"Why is it dangerous to fuck a dragon?" she asks, eyes wide. "You don't... shift in the middle, like accidentally or something, do you?"

A laugh-snort erupts from me and quickly fades. "Oh, man. I need to write a scene in my book where that happens."

"Ew, gross." She looks at me like I'm nuts. "Do *not* do that."

I lean forward and softly brush a kiss on her cheek. "I'm fully in control of all my parts while fucking, thank you very much."

Now that I'm close, her fingers wind into my hair. "Okay, you lied. You are *such* a tease."

I pull back and try to stay serious. "It's dangerous because I can't get you pregnant. Your body can't handle it. Not unless we're mated. So, we can't take any chances—"

"Have you heard of birth control? This little pill I take every day? It's this modern thing that, you know—"

"Even that could fail. Even condoms fail. It's a literal death sentence, Grace." It's not like I haven't taken the risk before, of course. Sex came with the Friday night parties, but every dragon is drilled in the proper use of condoms, and so far, no deadly pregnancies. But it *could* happen. And somehow the risk looms larger with Grace—partly because she's vulnerable and partly because I'm just so protective of her.

"Shit." She flops back on the bed and runs both hands through her hair, fanning out the long black tresses on my gray bedspread. "Wait." She looks up. "You said *unless we're mated.* What is that, exactly?" She props up again, intensely interested.

"That's a fusing of our souls."

"Wait... really?" Her eyes are wide. "Does it hurt?"

I smile. "No. In fact, I hear it's the most amazing sex you've ever had."

"Hold up. You lost me." She narrows her eyes. "You mean the mating is literally The Mating. Like having sex. But you can't have sex until you're mated. You realize none of this makes any sense, right?" I think she's just frustrated, which I am too, as evidenced by my cock straining to burst out of my jeans.

I lean in and kiss her softly on the lips. "Okay, listen up, and I'll try to use some words that make sense." I'm teasing her, but it's mostly an excuse to kiss her.

"You're the weird alien species here, not me."

"Hey!" I protest.

"I mean that in the best possible way."

I growl mock-frustration and dip down to nibble on her neck, holding her chin to the side to give me more complete access. "There are things I can do to you," I whisper along her skin. "We don't have to wait until we're mated."

She's squirming under my attention. "What... do you mean?" But she's definitely not asking me to stop.

I kiss up to her ear and nibble a little there, then pull back. My hand has found its way back to the softness of her belly. "I mean, I can make you come all day long—and I will, Grace; that's a promise I intend to keep—and you won't end up mated to me. There are two very specific things required for that." I have all her attention now. "First, you have to fall in love with me. And second, we have to make love, together, with our whole hearts. That's me, deep inside you, coming like I've never come before while giving you the best orgasm of your life.

That's when the magic happens—that's when our souls literally fuse."

Her breathing is a little erratic. "And then?"

"Then we can fuck all we like." I smirk and peck a kiss on her cheek.

She growls at me and tries to shove me away. "That's not what I meant!"

I don't move an inch. "Oh, and you'll turn into a dragon," I say casually.

She freezes in her struggle to push me away. "Me? *I* will turn into a dragon."

I nod. "Complete with the mated dragon's full arsenal—super strength, ability to teleport, venom lethal to the Vardigah. The whole package. Oh, and incredible sex. That's a perk, too."

She's grabbing hold of me again, but this time because she's struggling to sit up in the bed. "You are fucking with me."

"I am not. Sadly. But I'd be happy to." I slip my arms around her waist and pull her down, this time with her on top.

She's braced against my chest, staring down at me with an incredulous expression. "I can turn into a dragon."

"If we mate. Which, as I said—"

"With the big, sharp talons."

"Yes." Obviously. She's seen me in action.

"So, I can fucking kill the Vardigah if they come for me." She's suddenly deadly serious.

I scowl. "What? I mean... I guess?" I skim my hands up her arms, which are now rigid and locked, with her hands pressing into my chest. "I hope that never happens."

"But if it did, I would be prepared." She nods like this is what she wants, so I don't argue it any further. It's the truth. "Okay. Let's do it."

A smile tugs on my lips. "Which part, specifically?"

Her arms soften, and she peers into my eyes. "Let's get mated."

My smile fades. "It doesn't work that way—"

"But you said—"

"Grace, you have to be in love with me first." I give her arms a gentle squeeze.

"I love you."

Frustration swells up in me. "You can't just say it." I lift up and roll her back on the bed with me looming over her again. "The magic won't work unless it's real. We're fusing souls here—it's not something you can fake."

She purses her lips and squints up at me.

I try to banish the scowl on my face. "We can

mess around. I *will* make it worth your time. We don't have to mate right away. Or at all." I try to keep that last part light, but it's kind of a stab through the chest.

She frowns like she's considering it.

My heart squeezes—maybe all she wants is something casual. Not just now, but ever. Maybe there's just a whole lot of heartache ahead for me. One more failed dragon reporting back to Niko about how he fucked up his one and only chance to romance his soul mate—mainly because I'm an idiot and didn't even decide I *wanted* it until it was probably too late.

"I don't let just anyone on the couch," she says.

"I'm sorry?" I move a little to the side so I'm not pressuring her with my body anymore.

She turns to face me, propping her head up with her hand. "You're the only one I've let take Mari's spot on the couch." My eyebrows lift at the sudden shift, but before I can say anything, she adds, "I told you about my wish—to have my family back."

I nod, frowning, not sure where this is going.

"And I wanted *you* to write Michiko's story."

"Okay." But I shake my head a little. "I don't understand."

"I'm trying to tell you all the ways that I love you."

I blink and actually draw back. My heart thuds as I mentally race back over the things she's listed. "You let me in," I say, connecting the pieces.

"I don't let *anyone* in, Theo." She reaches up and touches her fingertips to my lips. "I didn't know you were my soul mate. I had no idea about any of the magic stuff. All I knew was that, when I was next to you, something settled inside me. I could be *me* with you. And that just doesn't happen, not for me. Not with almost anyone."

"I'm your personal Prozac." I smile a little, but my heart is racing.

"And I'm so very addicted to you." She says it softly and lifts up to follow it with a kiss. It's tender and sweet, and it's wrenching emotion out of me like I'm a damn sponge.

"Grace." But I'm choked up, words fleeing before the storm of all this feeling.

"I love you, you stupid dragon," she whispers between kisses. "Make love to me."

It turns me inside out. Grace is holding my face gently in her hands as she kisses me, sweetly, sensually, like she wants more than just what she can touch—*she wants all of me*. The writer. The dragon.

The fool who can't see what's right in front of him but eventually figures it out. *That I want all of her. Forever.*

"Are you sure?" It almost breaks me to ask, but I have to be certain. "There's no turning back, Grace. If we do this—"

"You're stuck with me." She pulls back far enough to look me in the eyes. She's daring me with them, as if to say, *I know what I'm getting into, but do you?*

I do. More than she knows.

I lean into kissing her, pressing her flat on the bed again. I'm on top of her, weighting her with my body, but not too much—just enough to know I mean every word of this. "You complete me, Grace Tanaka," I whisper, my cheek nuzzling hers. "Your soul is my soul. Your heart beats with mine. You are the greatest treasure I will ever have."

A shudder goes through her. A sharp intake of breath. And when I kiss her this time, neither of us is holding back. Her hands are in my hair. Mine seek her bare skin. She's arching up into me, and it's clear we have on way too many clothes. I lift off her, then pull us both up to our knees. I love *looking* at her—the smoothness of her skin, the delicate beauty of her face—but I need to see more. I lift off her shirt, then reach behind to release her bra. I stall out at the magnificence of her breasts—just the size to fit my hand, her nipple taut against my palm. She's tugging at my shirt, so I sacrifice touching her for a moment to yank that off, but then she's pulling at my jeans, which reminds me...

"Hang on." I pull her hand away and swing myself off the bed, going for the top drawer of the dresser with the speed of a man who has Grace waiting for him in bed. I pluck a condom out and hold it up. "Just to be safe." She nods and watches as I hold the edge of the package between my teeth and strip down fast out of my jeans and underwear. My cock's free for a moment, just long enough for me to rip the wrapping from the condom and sheath myself.

Her eyes are wide as I climb back on the bed. She still has her shorts on, so I lay her back again and quickly pull those off. Then I capture her ankle in my hand and start at her toes, kissing my way, long and slow along the slender beauty that is Grace's legs. She's squirming by the time I reach her sex, but she gasps when I go straight for it, lapping her sweetness and burrowing in. She's whimpering and crying, but I take my time, thoroughly exploring and tasting and teasing with the tip of my tongue just to hear her pleasure. When she bucks against me, cursing me out and grabbing my hair, I lock it down, my arm around her waist, holding her tight and lifting her sex into my mouth, adding my fingers to the mix. My thrusts match hers, my mouth locked onto her, and when she comes, it's the most beautiful blossoming I've tasted, her screams echoing around the room and her body convulsing around my fingers.

She slumps into the bed, spent.

I'm just getting started.

I slowly release her, soft kisses on her belly marking my goodbye, for the moment, to the sweet playtime between her legs.

When I look up, she's peering down at me between those two luscious breasts, each pointed at the sky and making my mouth ache. *"Holy fuck,* Theo," she breathes.

"That comes next," I say with a smirk, slowly sliding up her body. A shiver runs through me because *this is it*—either she truly loves me or she doesn't. I'll know soon enough. I will make love to her either way—I'm determined to rock Grace's world no matter what—but in the end, either we'll be mated dragons or...

I'll be one half of a heartbroken soul.

THIRTEEN

Grace

My mind is swimming in orgasm.

That doesn't make any sense, but the level of orgasm Theo gives with only his mouth and hands has made me leave the physical realm. I'm floating in pleasure, my entire being abuzz… and now he's sliding up my body, skin against skin, with hooded eyes that mean he's not even close to done.

Plus, there's that cock. I've seen it before, but not huge and stiff and pressing against my body. *How the fuck is that supposed to fit inside me?*

"It'll fit." Theo's looming above me, smirking.

"Oh, shit. Did I say that out loud?"

He laughs, and it shakes both of us, lying flat on the bed, him on top of me. *"Grace,"* he breathes, ducking his head down to nibble on my neck. "Do you know how much I've dreamed of this?" His hand reaches down, lifting my leg and spreading me wide. He's sliding against me, his hardness hitting right where it feels best.

"*Uhgn,* Theo." My fingers dig into his back.

He slides more, the full length of him against all my wanton wetness. With each pull back, his tip gets closer to my entrance. "Do you like that?"

"Yes." I'm breathless again, already feeling the ache of desire between my legs ramping up. He really is bigger than anyone I've had before, and that's saying something.

He shifts his weight and reaches to pull my other leg up. I'm spread and ready for him, but a flutter of nerves goes through me. What if this isn't the right choice? Do I know what I'm getting into? Theo shifts again, rubbing my inflamed nub and spiking pleasure through me.

"*Ah!*" I pant, clutching at him.

"Say it again," he whispers against my cheek. He's *so close* to entering me, but just sliding past, running roughshod over all my sensitive parts.

"Say *what?*" I gasp.

"That you love me." I hear the vulnerability in it.

I move my hands from desperately clutching at

his shoulders up to his hair, cradling and cuddling his head. "Oh, I love you, Theo," I breathe. "There's no doubt about that."

He pulls back a little and slows with the insane slide. "But there is doubt."

I peer up at him. Those beautiful blue eyes, so intelligent and kind. I loved those from the first moment I saw him. "You're just really *big,* okay? A girl's gotta wonder."

He grins and dips down to whisper, "We're made for each other, Grace." And then he slides down, positions his tip at my entrance, and with one swift stroke—

"Oh, *fuck!*" I arch up as he sinks all the way in. The feeling of stretch is insane.

He holds there a moment, cursing, back arched into me. Then he slides a hand under my bottom, lifting me, angling himself *deeper,* for fuck's sake.

"Oh, God… *Theo!*" If he goes any further, I'm going to drown in his cock.

He moans. "You're so perfect," he mutters. Then he pulls back slow—*and thrusts hard.*

I yelp and clutch at his shoulders.

"That's right," he pants as he pulls back. "Hold on, Grace. Hold onto me." Then he thrusts in again and again, and it's all I can do to keep a grip on him. Each stroke jolts a whimper out of me. It's not just that he's huge... there's some sizzle that's happening everywhere we touch. A spark, only like pure pleasure, and it's riding up and down his cock as he plunges into me, seating fully with each thrust. He's breathing hard through his teeth, with a soft grunting that's driving me insane. That and every time he bangs, a fresh spike of pleasure shoots through me. He growls and shifts position, pulling me to the side of the bed so that I'm half arched off it. I'm barely hanging on to him as he slams into me, completely relying on him to keep us on the bed. I'm whimpering and clutching, and he just picks up the pace. The tension is building, every muscle in me starting to quiver, but the sensitive spots he's banging, thrusting, wildly owning, most of all. "Grace!" he growls. "Fuck! Come for me. I'm... going to..." His thrusting becomes almost frantic, and then he buries himself deep. And the grinding feel of him, the hot pulsing inside me, tips me over the edge. All the quivers build to one body-shaking spasm of pleasure that wracks and wracks me... until I feel like I'm breaking wide open. I buck against him, cursing and calling out, and it's like I'm possessed, squirming under the shuddering weight of his body. His groaning goes on and on, and we're like one being made of pleasure and heat, writhing against each other because it's all just too much.

Then the wave passes, and we cling to each other, panting and not moving, lest we break the spell. I'm hanging half off the bed, the blood rushing to my head, but I could stay here forever, Theo deep inside me, his iron strength holding me over the precipice, his pleasure and mine both filling me.

I'm suffused with light and joy… and a whole lot of heat.

In fact, I think I've come down with insta-fever from Theo's red-hot love-making.

"Grace." His voice is soft, as gentle as his hands. He pulls me back up on the bed and lays my head on the pillow. "You okay?" He's peering at me.

"Yeah." I'm breathless. I put a hand to my forehead, and it comes away wet. I stare at it. "But sex with you is so fucking hot, I'm super gross and sweaty now."

His eyes fly open, and he puts a hand to my cheek. "You're so hot." He seems almost giddy about this.

I frown. "Not the way I want to be."

He smiles wide. Then he kisses me so thoroughly, I'm almost sure we're going to have more of the sexy sex. Which I honestly don't know if I'll survive. Then he pulls back and blows on me, like literal air all over my face. Which is goofy and weird, but it feels so good, I just close my eyes and enjoy the coolness. Then he kisses me again, and by the time he pulls back this time, I'm feeling a bit more normal. Well, normal in the heat department—totally tingly and amazing from the two blow-my-mind orgasms.

Suddenly, Theo eases off the bed and uses a tissue from somewhere to pull off the condom and dispose of it in a tiny wastebasket I hadn't even noticed. "No more of those," he says with a grin.

"I thought you said it was super dangerous..."

He just smirks and waits for me to put it together.

"Oh. Wait. Already?" I look down at my body. It looks no different. Well, it does—my breasts are slightly swollen, I'm wet everywhere down in the lady-parts area, and my skin is blotchy red from all the banging. But there's no visible sign of a lurking dragon beast. Then again, Theo's insanely sculpted body looks 100% male specimen, no hidden-dragon either.

He climbs up to standing at the side of the bed, offering his hand. "Come here."

I let him pull me up, and I have to brace on his chest for a moment because the head-rush is still there.

"You okay?" His sweet side is back in a flash. Amazingly, he's getting hard again. How is that even possible?

I plant my hands flat on his chest. "You *did* fuck me half off the bed. My blood's still figuring out where it should settle in my body."

He bites his lip and peers down at my body like he's trying to figure out which part to taste. Which, insanely, heats me up all over but especially in my abused lady-parts. How is *that* possible?

"I want to do very naughty things to you, Grace." His voice is so filled with need, my whole body reacts, automatically drawing closer to him. *"But,"* he adds, stepping back and holding my hands at arm's length, "I want to see your dragon first."

"How do I even…" I shrug helplessly as he lets go.

He glances around the bedroom. "You're right. There's no room here." He grabs my hand and hauls me out the bedroom door. There's more room in the living room, but I'm *buck naked.*

"What if your roommate comes back?" I'm crossing my legs and folding my arms over my chest.

"He's *not* coming back." Theo takes my hands and forces me to stop covering myself. Then he steps back. "My God, you're beautiful. How fucking lucky am I?" He says it with such sweet wonder, my whole body blushes in response. Then he moves on like it was nothing. "Okay, close your eyes and picture my dragon. Yours should be similar since we *are* mated." Then he beams that sunshine smile at me.

"You're sure?" I ask.

He frowns a tiny bit. "Can't you feel it?"

I feel a *million* things… but I think I know what he means. He's only a half dozen steps away, but there's a connection between us that somehow feels stretched. I didn't notice it when we were literally in each other's arms, much less when Theo was still *inside* me, but it's like I just know where he is. Physically. And the further away he is, the less I like it.

"Is this what it means to share a soul?" I ask, a little unsettled. "This feeling like we're connected?"

His frown deepens. "You don't like it."

"No, it's just… different." I probe the feeling a little more. "It's like what I felt before. The calm that came from being around you. Only stronger now. A lot stronger."

He looks relieved. "I feel it too." Then he rakes his gaze over my body. "I need you to hurry up and shift. Just so we know. I have plans." By which he means *plans for my body*.

That sends a tingling rush through me. I hurry up and close my eyes and envision being a dragon. I'm an actor, after all. *Becoming something different* is my entire gig. I think I'm failing until I open my eyes in frustration and find that my head is on the ceiling, and I have black glistening scales all over my arms… which are now legs.

Holy shit. I close my eyes and wish myself human again. I open them fast this time, relieved to see skin and fingers and feet.

Theo scoops me up and holds me to his chest, twirling me around. "Oh my God, you really did it!"

I laugh then have to grab hold of him because the dizziness is a little much. "Theo! Enough."

He stops twirling me and sets me down. His eyes are *on fire*. "Am I dreaming? Is this a dream, Grace?"

"Could be. I'm feeling kind of high. Probably not the right person to ask."

His hand cups my cheek. "If it's a dream, I don't want it to stop." His cock is certainly non-stop. I grab hold of it and stroke, thinking maybe a really good blow job might buy me a little time— I'm not sure if I can handle another Theo On Fire Orgasm™ right now.

He groans as I go down on my knees. His fingers wind into my hair. He's still huge, which presents a serious challenge. I'll have to use both hands, and I'm not getting much more than his tip in my mouth. Just as I'm working up some rhythm and devising some strategy, he growls and stops me, pulling me back up to standing.

"Sorry," he says, voice husky, "but that'll have to wait." Then he grabs my hand and hauls me back to the bedroom, closing the door then turning me to face it. He pins my hands above my head, and, suddenly, he's filling me, taking me from behind. I brace against his thrusts, but he's ramping up quickly, and it's all I can do to cling to the door. He's literally lifting me up with each thrust, my toes barely kissing the floor. The electric shock is zinging around my body again, and when Theo drops one hand to reach between me and the door, quickly finding my sensitive nub, I nearly shriek with the zap of magic there. It's impossibly good and wild and beautiful, this love we're making. And by the sounds Theo's making, he's nearly there. Already. Again.

How often can we do this? Do dragons just have insane stamina?

All thought is washed away in an orgasm that rushes up and blanks out everything.

Everything but this love I thought I'd never find and somehow found me instead.

FOURTEEN

Theo

MATED SEX IS *INSANE.*

Grace is face-down on the bed, prone, and I'm pounding hard enough to make the bed jump. I've always liked it a little on the rough side, and Grace —because we're fucking *made* for each other—can't get enough. All dragons have stamina, but this is nothing like the women I've romanced before. To be honest, even the wild ones never held much thrill for me. I just couldn't *connect* with them. But mated sex with Grace is off the charts in every way. We've been at it literally all night. No matter how rough— nothing crazy, just a lot of good, hard fucking—that mated dragon stamina brings us back for more. *And the magic*—my cock is literally sizzling with it. It's absolutely crazy. But the best part is the connection.

I'm wildly in love, I can't get enough of her, and the bond between us just sings.

Especially when she's squirming and crying out and coming around my cock.

Grace shivers under me, head to toe, the way she does when she comes, and the way she's clutching at the sheets, mouth open into the mattress, not making a sound... I know it's *really* good. I call it her silent scream. I thrust all the way through it, making it last until she finally goes limp under me. I'm still hard, but I have other plans yet —I just need to give her a minute.

If I'd known about this mated sex thing, I probably would have blown everything. As it is, it all worked out just right.

I pull out, slide up next to her on the bed, and drop a kiss on her cheek. "You look happy," I tease.

"I think you got me pregnant that time." Her voice is muffled, her face still half smashed into the mattress, and her eyes closed.

I push the hair out of her face so I can see her better. "Not likely." I lift up her limp hand and rest it on my steel-hard cock. Although the other dozens of times I've emptied dragon seed into her in the last twelve hours could have done it. No condoms anymore. And I've explained how, now that she's dragon, those birth-control pills aren't doing squat.

"You are a goddamn fuck machine." Her eyes are still closed, but she trails her hand up and down my cock, and oh yes… that feels nice.

"Only for you." I kiss the top of her head and angle so she can stroke me better. Even that is hot— everything with Grace is better than anything that's come before. Love is its own magic.

"Give me a minute," she says, "and I'll suck you until you cry."

"I did not cry."

The corner of her mouth twitches. "You did. It was so good you were begging me to stop."

"I was begging you to *finish*. That's a different thing. You're slightly evil when I'm tied up." We've only begun to explore the toys and bindings and things that are going to make the rest of my life a pleasure-filled haze. I know mated dragons go on honeymoons for a couple of weeks—I figured they were just in love. And happy. *Oh hell no*—it's because they need to do All The Sexual Things with this new mated pleasure-machine their bodies have become.

Grace opens her eyes and gives me a look that

pulses excitement straight down to my cock. "I think we should try that again."

"I think we should take a shower."

She gives a pointed look at my cock, then lifts an eyebrow like I'm crazy.

I grin. "Together."

"Ah." And as simple as that, she's up and leading me to the bathroom.

Once the water's warm, I lather her up and rinse her off. Then I take my sweet time washing that long hair of hers. My cock is dying for more, but the sensual part of this isn't to be missed. After she's rinsed, I let her do the same. I only make it halfway through that before I've got to bend her over into my favorite shower position—her one hand braced against the wall while the other holds the spray nozzle on her sex, vibrating her front while I pound in from behind. I know it rocks her hard, the dual-action, and the image of her all slippery, dripping wet and pleasuring herself, her hips firmly in my hands as I thrust, get me there in no time.

I gasp and sink deep, emptying myself into her as I brace against the wall.

It's a thousand-to-one odds that we're making a baby. Dragons are notoriously hard to get pregnant.

It might be years—decades even—before we can conceive.

I can't help but hope anyway.

She finishes with that small whimpering and shaking I love. I spend a long time standing in the shower and kissing her because there's no real hurry, but eventually, we climb out and towel off.

Then I make the radical suggestion that we get dressed.

She gives me a funny look. "Are we going somewhere?"

"I think we should." My serious tone stops her in combing her long, wet hair. "A honeymoon," I say with a small smile. "We should tell everyone we're going out of town. And I need to check in with Niko." My smile fades. "We still don't know how the Vardigah found you. I'd like to just get out of the city for a while."

She nods, but she's frowning. "I hadn't really thought about telling everyone yet. You know… about us."

I kiss her forehead. "We have time. Let's just call it a vacation."

We scavenge up some clothes—Grace has fresh things in her suitcase, but she'll need more soon. She scoops her phone off the floor where it was buried under the pile of clothing we abandoned twelve hours ago.

"I have, like, a thousand messages." She's tapping through them.

"Who from?"

"My mom." It takes her a moment as she reads, then she looks up. "Holy shit, you are not going to believe this!"

"What?" I pull on my shirt—it feels so strange to have clothes on again.

"My mom says my agent has been trying to get ahold of me." She's shaking her head, scrolling and reading fast. "She says *Chicago Scrubs* has been greenlit… and they want me back!"

"That's awesome!" But my chest is tight. We need to leave for a while. Do the Vardigah know where she works? Her family? How did they find us outside the exhibit? And how could they have put any of that together when they don't even speak human languages? I step closer and peer over her shoulder. "Does it say when they'll start shooting the next episode?"

"Oh, not for a few weeks." She waves that off. "Maybe longer. They probably don't even have a script."

I breathe a little easier. Then I take her cheeks

in my hands and kiss her, soft and sweet. "I knew they'd want you back. I bet you wowed them at the exhibit."

She shakes her head in wonder and pulls away from my kiss to keep reading on her phone. "My agent says they want me for…" She scrolls some more. "…a recurring Guest Star. *Theo.*" Her eyes are so lit up, it makes her even more beautiful.

"Congratulations." I grin and hug her tight.

She's practically vibrating in my arms, little leaps of happiness. And I couldn't be happier for her, except for my lingering concern about the Vardigah. Surely, we'll be able to sort that out before she has to shoot again.

I release her to finish dressing. She retreats to the bed, still only in a t-shirt, to read the rest of her messages.

"I want to check in with Niko," I remind her, taking a seat next to her. She nods, but she's still reading. "Together, Grace. We need to stay together until we get this sorted—"

She gasps, but she's not even listening to me— it's something on her phone. Then she grabs my arm. "Oh, my God. *Theo.*"

"What?" I smile, because she sounds excited, not alarmed. And I'm truly happy for her that all this—all the things she wanted—are coming through. The exhibit. Her family. The show.

She tears her gaze away from the phone and peers into my eyes. "The New York Times wrote up a review of the opening of the exhibit."

"Whoa, really? You're famous."

"No, *you're* famous."

I lean back. "What?" She shows me her phone, but it's just some long rambling text from her mom.

"Remember I told you I was keeping my mom in the loop?"

"Yeah." I scan the text. It says something about the paper, a writeup, some special editor she knows… I'm not following all of it.

"Well, she knows you wrote the script for the opening—"

"I *helped* write it. It's your story. Michiko's story."

"Whatever." Grace waves that off. "I told her you were a writer. That you had this amazing novel about dragons—"

"You *what?*" My alarm shoots through the roof. I actually stand up from the bed.

"It's *good*, Theo."

"You *showed* it to her?" My heart starts pounding.

"No." She puts her hands up and rises from the

bed. "I know that was just for me. Give me a little credit here."

I do—I trust Grace implicitly—but that doesn't keep my heart from racing.

She waves her phone at me. "But she told the reviewer and an editor friend of hers and…" She scans through the text. "I don't know, one thing led to another, and…" She looks up, a smile sneaking onto her face. "The editor wants to read your book."

"*What?*" I'm legit having a heart attack now. "Who?" I gasp.

She lifts her shoulders in a helpless shrug. "I don't know. Some lady at some publishing company."

"But it's not even done, Grace!"

"So, finish it." She puts her hands out like this is easy and obvious and…

Holy shit, an editor wants to see my book. I blink and slowly sit back down on the bed.

"This is so good, right?" Grace snuggles up next to me, wrapping her hands around my arm and resting her head on my shoulder.

"Yeah. I just… wow. Didn't see that coming."

"Plot twist!" she trills.

I shake my head. "You are not funny."

"I am so."

I extricate my arm from her grasp and wrap it around her. "Beautiful and feisty, yes. Fucking amazing in bed, 100%. But not a funny bone in your body."

"You're just jealous because I'm going to be a famous TV star." She bats her eyelids at me, and I want to rip her clothes off again. This will be a problem.

I smile. "I get to bang a movie star? Excellent."

"*Television* star. Small screen. That's where all the good stuff is now, anyway."

"That is true." I kiss her forehead and sigh. "We need to check in with Niko then get out of the city for a while. I'll… work on my book for the editor. I can't even believe those are words I'm saying with my mouth. And once we're settled on our honeymoon, we'll fuck *a lot*. Like, mostly, it will be fucking. And then, when we're sure it's safe, we'll come back." I pull back to see how she's taking this. "We'll be back in time for the shoot."

"I'll go anywhere with you, hot stuff." She says it with a smile, but the look in her eyes makes my heart soar.

I pull her in for a kiss. Just light and sweet because I'm way too close to starting something that will take an hour to finish, and we'll be right back to showering again. "You know, mating is far more permanent than marriage. We're literally fused together now. Your soul is my soul. If one of us dies, the other one goes."

She wrinkles up her nose. "Well, that's horrible."

I smile. "I still want to marry you, though. You know, make it official."

She sighs dramatically like this is a massive imposition. "I suppose."

I smile wider. "We could elope, but I think your mother might murder me."

She tips her head back and covers her face with both hands. "Oh, my God... I don't even want to think about it. My mother will be a *monster* with a wedding."

"Good thing we're doing the honeymoon first." I pull her up from the bed and swat her bare behind because she still hasn't put on pants. "Get dressed. I'll text Niko to tell him we're coming." She prances back to the pile of clothes and bends over, ostensibly looking for pants, but intentionally flashing me and wiggling her sweet ass while doing it.

I am the luckiest man alive.

I sigh and hunt for my phone. It's buried under the clothes as well.

Then I quickly text Niko. *Grace and I want to check in. See about the status of things.*

It takes a moment to come back. *Can be there in about 5.*

We'll come to you. I grin because he obviously hasn't guessed yet.

I'm back at the lair. That's a long way from NYC.

Grace is pulling on her white tennis shoes and looks ready to go, so I just leave Niko hanging. We don't need to bring much—we'll buy clothes wherever we end up. And anything else we need. The lair keeps several honeymoon cottages around the world, but I hear they're filling up fast.

"Pull together whatever you want to bring," I say to Grace as I gather up my purple notebooks and my laptop and find a bag to stash them in. I have everything else I need on my phone. Grace hardly brought anything from her apartment, but it's packed up and ready to go again. I sling the bag over my shoulder and take her hand in mine. "Ready for your first lesson in teleportation?"

She just shakes her head. "This is crazy."

I grin. "You can go anywhere you like—just focus on a person, place, or thing. The essence of it is that you're telegraphing your intention across magical space. As long as we're holding hands, only one has to have the intention. I'll bring us to Niko's office. But after that... where do you want to honeymoon?"

"I don't even know... your people, the dragons, are from Greece, right?"

"They're *your* people now. But we can't go to the old lair outside Athens. The Vardigah know where it is."

"How about the Greek Isles?"

"An island paradise where I can have you all to myself and fuck all day long? Absolutely." I squeeze her hand. "Close your eyes. It's a little less jarring that way."

She takes a deep breath and does it. I picture Niko's office, and my room shifts in a blink, replaced by the ornate wooden desk and bookshelves I remember.

Niko startles at our sudden appearance. "What the—" Then recognition dawns, and he smiles. "Well. I guess you figured it out."

I squirm a little with the reminder of my last visit—back when I was a pretty messed up dragon who thought an older dragon like Niko couldn't possibly understand what I was going through. Basically, an idiot. A well-intentioned idiot, but still. Which makes me realize I owe my father an apology. Or maybe just an introduction to my mate—the woman who will eventually give him grandchildren. Later, though. Before the wedding, for sure.

"Niko, this is Grace." They hardly got an introduction the last time, when I called him in to teleport us out of the alley and out of danger.

He comes around the desk, hand extended, all smiles. "It's a pleasure to meet you for real."

She shakes his hand. "This is all really weird."

He chuckles. "It gets easier. I'm sure my mate, Ember, would love to tell you all about being a mated dragon. Let me call her—"

I cut him off before he can get too far. "We're not staying, Niko. We want to go honeymooning. Greek Isles."

He nods and looks like he's suppressing a knowing smile. "Of course."

"Any luck on figuring out how the Vardigah found Grace?" I ask.

He grimaces. "No. But we've moved every one of the soul mates that we could convince to move. They're in safehouses or back here at the lair. We figure as long as there's no connection to their former lives, they can't be tracked down, kind of like being in witness protection for the moment, but we really have no idea how this is possible. How the Vardigah found them. We're working on it."

"Oh my God," Grace gasps, banging her fist on her forehead. "I forgot to check on Jayda!" She pulls out her phone and mumbles something like, *I'm the worst friend...*

I lift my chin to Niko. "Ree got her to a safe-house, right?"

"He should have." Niko frowns. "I've been so swamped... to be honest, I'm not sure he's checked in."

"Oh, no." Grace's whispered words draw us both. She's staring at her phone.

"What?" I ask, angling to see.

She turns her phone. It shows her text. *Jayda, Hey! Just checking in. I have so much to tell you!*

Jayda's response is stark. *How could you do this to me?*

"What did you *do?*" Grace demands.

Grace and Theo have their HEA, but there's more to the Broken Souls. Find out what happens next in *My Dragon Lover* (Broken Souls 5).

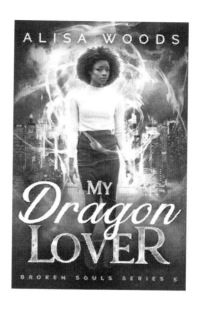

Get My Dragon Lover today!

Subscribe to Alisa's newsletter

for new releases and giveaways

http://smarturl.it/AWsubscribeBARDS

About the Author

Alisa Woods lives in the Midwest with her husband and family, but her heart will always belong to the beaches and mountains where she grew up. She writes sexy paranormal romances about complicated men and the strong women who love them. Her books explore the struggles we all have, where we resist—and succumb to—our most tempting vices as well as our greatest desires. No matter the challenge, Alisa firmly believes that hearts can mend and love will triumph over all.

www.AlisaWoodsAuthor.com

Printed in Great Britain
by Amazon

37478728R00149